Charles Fletcher Lummis

The Man who Married the Moon

And other Pueblo Indian Folk-stories

Charles Fletcher Lummis

The Man who Married the Moon
And other Pueblo Indian Folk-stories

ISBN/EAN: 9783744767316

Printed in Europe, USA, Canada, Australia, Japan

Cover: Foto ©Andreas Hilbeck / pixelio.de

More available books at **www.hansebooks.com**

THE MAN
WHO MARRIED
THE MOON

Charles F. Lummis

THE BOY IN THE HOUSE OF THE TRUES. (SEE PAGE 115.)

THE MAN WHO MARRIED
THE MOON

AND OTHER PUEBLO INDIAN FOLK-STORIES

BY

CHARLES F. LUMMIS

AUTHOR OF "SOME STRANGE CORNERS OF OUR COUNTRY"
"A NEW MEXICO DAVID," ETC.

NEW YORK
THE CENTURY CO.
1894

THE DE VINNE PRESS.

CONTENTS

		PAGE
INTRODUCTION: THE BROWN STORY-TELLERS		1
I	THE ANTELOPE BOY	12
II	THE COYOTE AND THE CROWS	22
III	THE WAR-DANCE OF THE MICE	24
IV	THE COYOTE AND THE BLACKBIRDS	27
V	THE COYOTE AND THE BEAR	30
VI	THE FIRST OF THE RATTLESNAKES	34
VII	THE COYOTE AND THE WOODPECKER	49
VIII	THE MAN WHO MARRIED THE MOON	53
IX	THE MOTHER MOON	71
X	THE MAKER OF THE THUNDER-KNIVES	74
XI	THE STONE-MOVING SONG	82
XII	THE COYOTE AND THE THUNDER-KNIFE	84
XIII	THE MAGIC HIDE-AND-SEEK	87
XIV	THE RACE OF THE TAILS	99
XV	HONEST BIG-EARS	103
XVI	THE FEATHERED BARBERS	106
XVII	THE ACCURSED LAKE	108
XVIII	THE MOQUI BOY AND THE EAGLE	122
XIX	THE NORTH WIND AND THE SOUTH WIND	127
XX	THE TOWN OF THE SNAKE-GIRLS	130
XXI	THE DROWNING OF PECOS	137

PAGE

XXII   THE ANTS THAT PUSHED ON THE SKY   147

XXIII THE MAN WHO WOULD N'T KEEP SUNDAY   161

XXIV   THE BRAVE BOBTAILS   169

XXV   THE REVENGE OF THE FAWNS   178

XXVI   THE SOBBING PINE   194

XXVII THE QUÈRES DIANA   200

XXVIII A PUEBLO BLUEBEARD   203

XXIX   THE HERO TWINS   206

XXX   THE HUNGRY GRANDFATHERS   215

XXXI   THE COYOTE   222

XXXII DOCTOR FIELD-MOUSE   232

LIST OF ILLUSTRATIONS

PAGE

The Boy in the House of the Trues   FRONTISPIECE

"As I come in, kindly old Tata Lorenso is just beginning a Story"   7

The Coyote ·carries the Baby to the Antelope Mother   15

Rain falls on Pée-k'hoo   18

"The two Runners came sweeping down the Homestretch, straining every Nerve"   20

"As He caught the Hoop He was instantly changed into a poor Coyote!"   37

"Coyote, are you People?"   41

"As He seized it He was changed from a tall young Man into a great Rattlesnake"   45

The Coyotes at Supper with the Woodpeckers   50

The Isleta Girls grinding Corn with the "Mano" on the "Metate"   56

The Moon-Maiden   57

The Yellow-Corn-Maidens throwing Meal at the pearl "Omate"   59

The Grief of Nah-chu-rú-chu   65

"The Witch made Herself very small, and went behind the Foot of a big Crane"   95

ix

PAGE

THE HUNTER AND THE LAKE-MAN   111

THE CURSING OF THE LAKE   119

SOUTH, EAST, NORTH, AND WEST IN SEARCH OF KAHP-
TOO-ÓO-YOO   153

KAHP-TOO-ÓO-YOO CALLING THE RAIN   158

THE WOLF, AND THE COYOTE WITH THE TOOTHACHE   183

THE WOLF MEETS THE BOYS PLAYING WITH THEIR
BOWS AND ARROWS   187

"THE FAWNS APPEARED SUDDENLY, AND AT SIGHT OF
THEM THE WOLF DROPPED THE SPOONFUL OF SOUP " 191

"THERE THEY STOOD SIDE BY SIDE "   .   225

"'HOW SHALL I GET IT?' SAID THE COYOTE "   229

These illustrations are from drawings by George Wharton Edwards,
after photographs by the author.

TÉE-WAHN FOLK-STORIES

THE BROWN STORY-TELLERS

FANCY that if almost any of us were asked, "When did people begin to make fairy stories?" our first thought would be, "Why, of course, after mankind had become civilized, and had invented writing." But in truth the making of myths, which is no more than a dignified name for "fairy stories," dates back to the childhood of the human race.

Long before Cadmus invented letters (and I fear Cadmus himself was as much of a myth as was his dragon's-teeth harvest), long before there were true historians or poets, there were fairy stories and story-tellers. And to-day, if we would seek the place where fairy stories most flourish, we must go, not to the nations whose countless educated minds are now devoted to story-telling for the young, but to peoples who have no books, no magazines, no alphabets — even no pictures.

Of all the aboriginal peoples that remain in North

America, none is richer in folk-lore than the Pueblo Indians of New Mexico, who are, I believe, next to the largest of the native tribes left in the United States. They number nine, thousand souls. They have nineteen "cities" (called pueblos, also) in this Territory, and seven in Arizona; and each has its little outlying colonies. They are not cities in size, it is true, for the largest (Zuñi) has only fifteen hundred people, and the smallest only about one hundred; but cities they are, nevertheless. And each city, with its fields, is a wee republic — twenty-six of the smallest, and perhaps the oldest, republics in the world; for they were already such when the first European eyes saw America. Each has its governor, its congress, its sheriffs, war-captains, and other officials who are elected annually; its laws, unwritten but unalterable, which are more respected and better enforced than the laws of any American community; its permanent and very comfortable houses, and its broad fields, confirmed first by Spain and later by patents of the United States.

The architecture of the Pueblo houses is quaint and characteristic. In the remote pueblos they are as many as six stories in height — built somewhat in the shape of an enormous terraced pyramid. The Pueblos along the Rio Grande, however, have felt the influence of Mexican customs, and their houses have but one and two stories. All their buildings, including the huge, quaint church which each pueblo has, are made of stone plastered with adobe mud, or of great, sun-dried bricks of adobe. They are the most comfortable dwellings in the Southwest — cool in summer and warm in winter.

The Pueblos are divided into six tribes, each speaking a distinct language of its own. Isleta, the quaint village where I lived five years, in an Indian house, with Indian neighbors, and under Indian laws, is the southernmost of the pueblos, the next largest of them all, and the chief city of the Tée-wahn tribe.[1] All the languages of the Pueblo tribes are exceedingly difficult to learn.

Besides the cities now inhabited, the ruins of about fifteen hundred other pueblos — and some of them the noblest ruins in the country — dot the brown valleys and rocky mesa-tops of New Mexico. All these ruins are of stone, and are extremely interesting. The implacable savages by whom they were hemmed in made necessary the abandonment of hundreds of pueblos; and this great number of ruins does not indicate a vast ancient population. The Pueblos *never* counted above 30,000 souls.

The Pueblo Indians have for nearly two centuries given no trouble to the European sharers of their domain; but their wars of defense against the savage tribes who surrounded them completely — with the Apaches, Navajos, Comanches, and Utes — lasted until a very few years ago. They are valiant fighters for their homes, but prefer any honorable peace. They are not indolent, but industrious — tilling their farms, tending their stock, and keeping all their affairs in order. The women own the houses and their contents, and do not work outside; and the men control the fields and crops. An unhappy home is almost an unknown thing among them; and the universal affection of parents for

1 Spelled Tigua by Spanish authors.

children and respect of children for parents are extraordinary. I have never seen a child unkindly treated, a parent saucily addressed, or a playmate abused, in all my long and intimate acquaintance with the Pueblos.

Isleta lies on the Atlantic and Pacific Railroad, upon the western bank of the Rio Grande, on a lava promontory which was once an island — whence the town takes its Spanish name. Its Tée-wahn title is Shee-eh-whíb-bak.[1] Its population, according to the census taken in 1891, is a little less than twelve hundred. It is nearly surrounded by fertile vineyards, orchards of peaches, apricots, apples, cherries, plums, pears, and quinces, and fields of corn, wheat, beans, and peppers, all owned by my dusky neighbors. The pueblo owns over one hundred and ten thousand acres of land, the greater part of which is reserved for pasturing horses and cattle.

The people of Isleta are, as a rule, rather short in stature, but strongly built. All have a magnificent depth and breadth of chest, and a beautifully confident poise of the head. Most of the men are very expert hunters, tireless runners, and fine horsemen. Besides ordinary hunting they have communal hunts—for rabbits in the spring, for antelope and deer in the fall — thoroughly organized, in which great quantities of game are killed.

Their amusements are many and varied. Aside from the numerous sacred dances of the year, their most important occasions, they have various races

---

[1] The name means "Knife-laid-on-the-ground-to-play-*whib*." *Whib* is an aboriginal foot-race in which the runners have to carry a stick with their toes. The name was perhaps suggested by the knife-like shape of the lava ridge on which the pueblo is built.

which call for great skill and endurance, quaint social enjoyments, and games of many kinds, some of which are quite as difficult as chess. They are very fair weavers and pottery-makers. The women are good housewives, and most of them excellent seamstresses.

Yet, with all this progress in civilization, despite their mental and physical acuteness and their excellent moral qualities, the Tée-wahn are in some things but overgrown children. Their secret inner religion[1] is one of the most complicated systems on earth. Besides the highest deities, all the forces of nature, all animals, as well as many things that are inanimate, are invested by them with supernatural powers. They do not worship idols, but images and tokens of unseen powers are revered. They do nothing without some reason, generally a religious one, and whatever they observe they can explain in their own superstitious way. Every custom they have and every belief they own has a reason which to them is all-sufficient; and for each they have a story. There is no duty to which a Pueblo child is trained in which he has to be content with the bare command, "Do thus"; for each he learns a fairy tale designed to explain how people first came to know that it was right to do thus, and detailing the sad results which befell those who did otherwise.

It is from this wonderful folk-lore of the Téewahn that I have learned—after long study of the people, their language, customs, and myths—and

[1] For they are all devout, if not entirely understanding, members of a Christian church; but keep also much of their prehistoric faiths.

taken, unchanged and unembellished, this series of Indian fairy tales. I have been extremely careful to preserve, in my translations, the exact Indian *spirit.* An absolutely literal translation would be almost unintelligible to English readers, but I have taken no liberties with the real meaning.

The use of books is not only to tell, but to preserve; not only for to-day, but for ever. What an Indian wishes to perpetuate must be saved by tongue and ear, by "telling-down," as were the world's first histories and poems. This oral transmission from father to son is of sacred importance with the natives. Upon it depends the preservation of the amusements, the history, the beliefs, the customs, and the laws of their nation. A people less observant, less accurate of speech and of memory, would make a sad failure of this sort of record; but with them it is a wonderful success. The story goes down from generation to generation, almost without the change of a word. The fact that it is told in fixed metrical form—a sort of blank verse —helps the memory.

Here in Isleta, the quaint pueblo of the Téc-wahn, I became deeply interested not only in the folk-stories themselves, but also in the manner of handing them down. Winter is the season for story-telling. Then the thirsty fields no longer cry for water, the irrigating-ditches have ceased to gnaw at their banks, and the men are often at leisure. Then, of an evening, if I go over to visit some *vecino* (neighbor), I am likely to find, in the great adobe living-room, a group of very old men and very young boys gathered about the queer little

"AS I COME IN, KINDLY OLD TATA LORENSO IS JUST BEGINNING A STORY."

corner fireplace with its blazing upright sticks. They, too, have come a-visiting. The young men are gathered in another corner by themselves, eating roasted corn, and talking in whispers so as not to disturb their elders, for respect to age is the corner-stone of all Indian training. They are not required to listen to the stories, being supposed to know them already.

If in the far, sweet days when I stood at my grandmother's knee, and shivered over "Bluebeard," or thrilled at "Jack the Giant-killer," some one could have shown us a picture of me as I was to be listening to other fairy tales twenty-five years later, I am sure that her eyes would have opened wide as mine. Certainly neither of us ever dreamed that, thousands of miles from the old New England fireplace, when the dear figures that sat with me before its blazing forestick had long been dust, I would be sitting where I am to-night and listening to the strange, dark people who are around me.

The room is long and low, and overhead are dark, round rafters — the trunks of straight pine-trees that used to purr on the sides of the most famous mountain in New Mexico. The walls are white as snow, and you would never imagine that they are built only of cut sods, plastered over and whitewashed. The floor is of adobe clay, packed almost as hard as a rock, and upon it are bright-hued blankets, woven in strange figures. Along the walls are benches, with wool mattresses rolled up and laid upon them. By and by these will be spread upon the floor for beds, but just now they

serve as cushioned seats.   Over in a corner are
strange earthen jars of water, with little gourd dippers floating, and here and there upon the wall
hang bows and arrows in sheaths of the tawny hide
of the mountain lion ; queer woven belts of red and
green, and heavy necklaces of silver and coral, with
charms of turquoise — the stone that stole its color
from the sky.

There is a fireplace, too, and we are gathered all
about it, a dozen or more — for I have become an
old friend here.   But it is not like the fireplace
where the little sister and I used to roast our apples and pop our corn.   A wee hearth of clay rises
a few inches from the floor ; a yard above it hangs
the chimney, like a big white hood ; and a little
wall, four feet high, runs from it out into the room,
that the wind from the outer door may not blow
the ashes.   There is no big front log, but three or
four gnarled cedar sticks, standing on one end,
crackle loudly.

Some of us are seated on benches, and upon the
floor.   His back against the wall, squats my host,
who is just going to begin another fairy story.
Such a wee, withered, wrinkled old man !   It seems
as though the hot winds of the Southwest had dried
him as they dry the forgotten last year's apples
that shrivel here and there upon lonely boughs.
He must be a century old.   His children, grandchildren,   great-grandchildren,   and   great-great-
grandchildren are all represented here to-night.
Yet his black eyes are like a hawk's, under their
heavy brows, and his voice is musical and deep.
I have never heard a more eloquent story-teller,

and I have heard some famous ones.   I can tell you the words, but not the impressive tones, the animation of eye and accent, the eloquent gestures of this venerable Indian as he tells — what?   An Indian telling fairy stories?

Yes, indeed.   He is the very man to tell them. If this dusky old playground for wrinkles, who never saw the inside of a book, could write out all the fairy stories he knows, Webster's Unabridged Dictionary would hardly hold them.   His father and his father's father, and so on back for count-less centuries, have handed down these stories by telling, from generation to generation, just as Tata' Lorenso is telling his great-great-grandsons to-night.   When these boys grow up, they will tell these stories to their sons and grandsons; and so the legends will pass on and on, so long as there shall be a Tée-wahn Indian left in all New Mexico.

But Lorenso is ready with his story.   He pauses only to make a cigarette from the material in my pouch (they call me *Por todos*, because I have to-bacco " for all "), explains for my benefit that this is a story of the beginning of Isleta, pats the head of the chubby boy at his knee, and begins again.

1 " Father."

I

ONCE upon a time there were two towns of the Tée-wahn, called Nah-bah-tóo-too-ee (white village) and Nah-choo-rée-too-ee (yellow village). A man of Nah-bah-tóo-too-ee and his wife were attacked by Apaches while out on the plains one day, and took refuge in a cave, where they were besieged. And there a boy was born to them. The father was killed in an attempt to return to his village for help; and starvation finally forced the mother to crawl forth by night seeking roots to eat. Chased by the Apaches, she escaped to her own village, and it was several days before she could return to the cave—only to find it empty.

The baby had begun to cry soon after her departure. Just then a Coyote[1] was passing, and heard. Taking pity on the child, he picked it up and carried it across the plain until he came to a herd of antelopes. Among them was a Mother-Antelope that had lost her fawn; and going to her the Coyote said:

"Here is an *ah-bóo* (poor thing) that is left by its people. Will you take care of it?"

[1] The small prairie-wolf.

The Mother-Antelope, remembering her own baby, with tears said " Yes," and at once adopted the tiny stranger, while the Coyote thanked her and went home.

So the boy became as one of the antelopes, and grew up among them until he was about twelve years old. Then it happened that a hunter came out from Nah-bah-tóo-too-ee for antelopes, and found this herd. Stalking them carefully, he shot one with an arrow. The rest started off, running like the wind; but ahead of them all, as long as they were in sight, he saw a boy! The hunter was much surprised, and, shouldering his game, walked back to the village, deep in thought. Here he told the Cacique[1] what he had seen. Next day the crier was sent out to call upon all the people to prepare for a great hunt, in four days, to capture the Indian boy who lived with the antelopes.

While preparations were going on in the village, the antelopes in some way heard of the intended hunt and its purpose. The Mother-Antelope was very sad when she heard it, and at first would say nothing. But at last she called her adopted son to her and said: " Son, you have heard that the people of Nah-bah-tóo-too-ee are coming to hunt. But they will not kill us; all they wish is to take you. They will surround us, intending to let all the antelopes escape from the circle. You must follow me where I break through the line, and your real mother will be coming on the northeast side in a white *manta* (robe). I will pass close to her, and you must stagger and fall where she can catch you."

[1] The highest religious official.

2

On the fourth day all the people went out upon the plains. They found and surrounded the herd of antelopes, which ran about in a circle when the hunters closed upon them. The circle grew smaller, and the antelopes began to break through; but the hunters paid no attention to them, keeping their eyes upon the boy. At last he and his antelope mother were the only ones left, and when she broke through the line on the northeast he followed her and fell at the feet of his own human mother, who sprang forward and clasped him in her arms.

Amid great rejoicing he was taken to Nah-bah-tóo-too-ee, and there he told the *principales*[1] how he had been left in the cave, how the Coyote had pitied him, and how the Mother-Antelope had reared him as her own son.

It was not long before all the country round about heard of the Antelope Boy and of his marvelous fleetness of foot. You must know that the antelopes never comb their hair, and while among them the boy's head had grown very bushy. So the people called him *Pée-hleh-o-wah-wée-deh* (big-headed little boy).

Among the other villages that heard of his prowess was Nah-choo-rée-too-ee, all of whose people "had the bad road."[2] They had a wonderful runner named *Pée-k'hoo* (Deer-foot), and very soon they sent a challenge to Nah-bah-tóo-too-ee for a championship race. Four days were to be given for preparation, to make bets, and the like.

---

[1] The old men who are the congress of the pueblo.
[2] That is, were witches.

THE COYOTE CARRIES THE BABY TO THE ANTELOPE MOTHER.

The race was to be around the world.[1] Each village was to stake all its property and the lives of all its people on the result of the race. So powerful were the witches of Nah-choo-rée-too-ee that they felt safe in proposing so serious a stake; and the people of Nah-bah-tóo-too-ee were ashamed to decline the challenge.

The day came, and the starting-point was surrounded by all the people of the two villages, dressed in their best. On each side were huge piles of ornaments and dresses, stores of grain, and all the other property of the people. The runner for the yellow village was a tall, sinewy athlete, strong in his early manhood; and when the Antelope Boy appeared for the other side, the witches set up a howl of derision, and began to strike their rivals and jeer at them, saying, "Pooh! We might as well begin to kill you now! What can that *óo-deh* (little thing) do?"

At the word "*Hái-ko!*" ("Go!") the two runners started toward the east like the wind. The Antelope Boy soon forged ahead; but Deer-foot, by his witchcraft, changed himself into a hawk and flew lightly over the lad, saying, "*We* do this way to each other!"[2] The Antelope Boy kept running, but his heart was very heavy, for he knew that no feet could equal the swift flight of the hawk.

1 The Pueblos believed it was an immense plain whereon the racers were to race over a square course — to the extreme east, then to the extreme north, and so on, back to the starting-point.

2 A common Indian taunt, either good-natured or bitter, to the loser of a game or to a conquered enemy.

But just as he came half-way to the east, a Mole came up from its burrow and said:

"My son, where are you going so fast with a sad face?"

The lad explained that the race was for the

RAIN FALLS ON PÉE-K'HOO.

property and lives of all his people; and that the witch-runner had turned to a hawk and left him far behind.

"Then, my son," said the Mole, "I will be he that shall help you. Only sit down here a little while, and I will give you something to carry."

The boy sat down, and the Mole dived into the hole, but soon came back with four cigarettes.[1]

Holding them out, the Mole said, "Now, my son, when you have reached the east and turned north, smoke one; when you have reached the north and turn west, smoke another; when you turn south, another, and when you turn east again, another. *Hái-ko!*"

The boy ran on, and soon reached the east. Turning his face to the north he smoked the first cigarette. No sooner was it finished than he became a young antelope; and at the same instant a furious rain began. Refreshed by the cool drops, he started like an arrow from the bow. Half-way to the north he came to a large tree; and there sat the hawk, drenched and chilled, unable to fly, and crying piteously.

"Now, friend, *we* too do this to each other," called the boy-antelope as he dashed past. But just as he reached the north, the hawk — which had become dry after the short rain — caught up and passed him, saying, "We too do this to each other!" The boy-antelope turned westward, and smoked the second cigarette; and at once another terrific rain began.[2] Half-way to the west he again passed the hawk shivering and crying in a tree,

1 These are made by putting a certain weed called *pee-én-hleh* into hollow reeds.

2 I should state, by the way, that the cigarette plays an important part in the Pueblo folk-stories, — they never had the pipe of the Northern Indians, — and all rain-clouds are supposed to come from its smoke.

and unable to fly; but as he was about to turn to the south, the hawk passed him with the customary taunt. The smoking of the third cigarette brought another storm, and again the antelope passed the wet hawk half-way, and again the hawk dried its feathers in time to catch up and pass him as he was turning to the east for the home-stretch. Here again the boy-antelope stopped and smoked a cigarette — the fourth and last. Again a short,

"THE TWO RUNNERS CAME SWEEPING DOWN THE HOME-STRETCH, STRAINING EVERY NERVE."

hard rain came, and again he passed the water-bound hawk half-way.

Knowing the witchcraft of their neighbors, the people of Nah-bah-tóo-too-ee had made the condition that, in whatever shape the racers might run the rest of the course, they must resume human form upon arrival at a certain hill upon the fourth turn, which was in sight of the goal. The last wetting of the hawk's feathers delayed it so that the antelope reached the hill just ahead; and there, resuming their natural shapes, the two runners came sweeping down the home-stretch, straining every nerve. But the Antelope Boy gained at each stride. When they saw him, the witch-people felt confident that he was their champion, and again began to push, and taunt, and jeer at the others. But when the little Antelope Boy sprang lightly across the line, far ahead of Deer-foot, their joy turned to mourning.

The people of Nah-bah-tóo-too-ee burned all the witches upon the spot, in a great pile of corn; but somehow one escaped, and from him come all the witches that trouble us to this day.

The property of the witches was taken to Nah-bah-tóo-too-ee; and as it was more than that village could hold, the surplus was sent to Shee-eh-whíb-bak (Isleta), where we enjoy it to this day; and later the people themselves moved here. And even now, when we dig in that little hill on the other side of the *charco* (pool), we find charred corn-cobs, where our forefathers burned the witch-people of the yellow village.

During Lorenso's story the black eyes of the boys have never left his face; and at every pause they have made the customary response, "Is that so?" to show their attention; while the old men have nodded approbation, and smoked in deep silence.

Now Lorenso turns to Desiderio,[1] who is far more wrinkled even than he, and says, "You have a tail, brother." And Desiderio, clearing his throat and making a new cigarette with great impressiveness, begins: "My sons, do you know why the Coyote and the Crows are always at war? No? Then I will tell you."

[1] Pronounced Day-see-dáy-ree-oh.

II

THE COYOTE AND THE CROWS

ONCE on a time many Káh-ahn lived in the edge of some woods. A little out into the plain stood a very large tree, with much sand under it. One day a Coyote was passing, and heard the Crows singing and dancing under this tree, and came up to watch them. They were dancing in a circle, and each Crow had upon his back a large bag.

"Crow-friends, what are you doing?" asked the Coyote, who was much interested.

"Oh, we are dancing with our mothers," said the Crows.

"How pretty! And will you let me dance, too?" asked the Coyote of the *too-whit-lah-wid-deh* crow (captain of the dance).

"Oh, yes," replied the Crow. "Go and put your mother in a bag and come to the dance."

The Coyote went running home. There his old mother was sitting in the corner of the fireplace. The stupid Coyote picked up a stick and struck her on the head, and put her in a bag, and hurried back to the dance with her.

The Crows were dancing merrily, and singing: "*Ai nana, que-ée-rah, que-ée-rah.*" ("Alas, Mama!

you are shaking, you are shaking!") The Coyote
joined the dance, with the bag on his back, and
sang as the Crows did:

"*Ai nana, que-ée-rah, que-ée-rah.*" [1]

But at last the Crows burst out laughing, and
said, "What do you bring in your bag?"

"My mother, as you told me," replied the Coyote, showing them.

Then the Crows emptied their bags, which were
filled with nothing but sand, and flew up into the
tree, laughing.

The Coyote then saw that they had played him
a trick, and started home, crying "*Ai nana!*"
When he got home he took his mother from the
bag and tried to set her up in the chimney-corner,
always crying, "*Ai nana*, why don't you sit up as
before?" But she could not, for she was dead.
When he found that she could not sit up any more,
he vowed to follow the Crows and eat them all the
rest of his life; and from that day to this he has
been hunting them, and they are always at war.

As Desiderio concludes, the old men hitch their
blankets around their shoulders. "No more stories
to-night?" I ask; and Lorenso says:

"*In-dáh* (no). Now it is to go to bed. *Tóo-kwai*
(come)," to the boys. "Good night, friends. Another time, perhaps."

And we file out through the low door into the
starry night.

---

[1] *Ai nana* is an exclamation always used by mourners.

III

THE WAR-DANCE OF THE MICE

TO-NIGHT it is withered Diego[1] who begins with his story, in the musical but strange Tée-wahn tongue, of "Shée-choon t'o-ah-fuar." Serious as that looks, it means only "the war-dance of the Mice."

Once upon a time there was war between the people of Isleta and the Mice. There was a great battle, in which the Tée-wahn killed many Mice and took their scalps. Then the Tée-wahn returned to their village, and the warriors went into the *estufa* (sacred council-chamber) to prepare themselves by fasting for the great scalp-dance in twelve days. While the warriors were sitting inside, the Mice came secretly by night to attack the town, and their spies crept up to the *estufa*. When all the Tée-wahn warriors had fallen asleep, the Mice came stealing down the big ladder into the room, and creeping from sleeper to sleeper, they gnawed every bowstring and cut the feathers from the arrows and the strap of every sling. When this was done, the Mice raised a terrible war-whoop and rushed upon the warriors, brandishing their

[1] Pronounced Dee-áy-go.

spears.   The Tée-wahn woke and caught up their
bows and arrows, but only to find them useless.
So the warriors could do nothing but run from their
tiny foes, and up the ladder to the roof they rushed
pell-mell and thence fled to their homes, leaving
the Mice victorious.

The rest of the town made such fun of the warriors that they refused to return to the fight; and
the elated Mice held a public dance in front of the
estufa.   A brave sight it was, the army of these
little people, singing and dancing and waving their
spears.   They were dressed in red blankets, with
leather leggings glistening with silver buttons from
top to bottom, and gay moccasins.   Each had two
eagle feathers tied to the top of his spear — the
token of victory.   And as they danced and marched
and counter-marched, they sang exultingly:

> *Shée-oh-pah ch'-ót-im!*
> *Neh-máh-hlee-oh ch'-ot-im!*
> *Hló-tu feé-ny p'-óh-teh!*

over and over again — which means

> Quick we cut the bowstring!
> Quick we cut the sling-strap!
> We shaved the arrow-feathers off!

For four days they danced and sang, and on the
night of the fourth day danced all night around
a big bonfire.   The next morning they marched
away.   That was the time when the Mice conquered men; and that is the reason why we have
never been able to drive the Mice out of our homes
to this day.

3

"Is *that* the reason?" ask all the boys, who have been listening with big black eyes intent.

"That is the very reason," says withered Diego. "Now, *compadre* Antonio, there is a tail to you."

Antonio, thus called upon, cannot refuse. Indian etiquette is very strict upon this point — as well as upon all others. So he fishes in his memory for a story, while the boys turn expectant faces toward him. He is not nearly so wrinkled as Diego, but he is very, very old, and his voice is a little tremulous at first. Wrapping his blanket about him, he begins:

Then I will tell you why the Coyote and the Blackbirds are enemies—for once they were very good friends in the old days.

IV

ONCE upon a time a Coyote lived near an open wood. As he went to walk one day near the edge of the wood, he heard the Blackbirds (the Indian name means "seeds of the prairie") calling excitedly:

"Bring my bag! Bring my bag! It is going to hail!"

The Coyote, being very curious, came near and saw that they all had buckskin bags to which they were tying lassos, the other ends of which were thrown over the boughs of the trees. Very much surprised, the Coyote came to them and asked:

"Blackbird-friends, what are you doing?"

"Oh, friend Coyote," they replied, "we are making ourselves ready, for soon there will be a very hard hail-storm, and we do not wish to be pelted to death. We are going to get into these bags and pull ourselves up under the branches, where the hail cannot strike us."

"That is very good," said the Coyote, "and I would like to do so, too, if you will let me join you."

"Oh, yes! Just run home and get a bag and a lasso, and come back here and we will help you," said the Pah-táhn, never smiling.

So the Coyote started running for home, and got a large bag and a lasso, and came back to the Blackbirds, who were waiting. They fixed the rope and bag for him, putting the noose around the neck of the bag so that it would be closed tight when the rope was pulled. Then they threw the end of the lasso over a strong branch and said:

"Now, friend Coyote, you get into your bag first, for you are so big and heavy that you cannot pull yourself up, and we will have to help you."

The Coyote crawled into the bag, and all the Blackbirds taking hold of the rope, pulled with all their might till the bag was swung clear up under the branch. Then they tied the end of the lasso around the tree so the bag could not come down, and ran around picking up all the pebbles they could find.

"Mercy! How the hail comes!" they cried excitedly, and began to throw stones at the swinging bag as hard as ever they could.

"Mercy!" howled the Coyote, as the pebbles pattered against him. "But this is a terrible storm, Blackbird-friends! It pelts me dreadfully! And how are you getting along?"

"It is truly very bad, friend Coyote," they answered, "but you are bigger and stronger than we, and ought to endure it." And they kept pelting him, all the time crying and chattering as if they, too, were suffering greatly from the hail.

"Ouch!" yelled the Coyote. "That one hit me very near the eye, friends! I fear this evil storm will kill us all!"

"But be brave, friend," called back the Blackbirds. "We keep our hearts, and so should you, for you are much stronger than we." And they pelted him all the harder.

So they kept it up until they were too tired to throw any more; and as for the Coyote, he was so bruised and sore that he could hardly move. Then they untied the rope and let the bag slowly to the ground, and loosened the noose at the neck and flew up into the trees with sober faces.

"Ow!" groaned the Coyote, "I am nearly dead!" And he crawled weeping and groaning from the bag, and began to lick his bruises. But when he looked around and saw the sun shining and the ground dry, and not a hailstone anywhere, he knew that the Blackbirds had given him a trick, and he limped home in a terrible rage, vowing that as soon as ever he got well he would follow and eat the Blackbirds as long as he lived. And ever since, even to this day, he has been following them to eat them, and that is why the Coyote and the Black-birds are always at war.

"Is that so?" cried all the boys in chorus, their eyes shining like coals.

"Oh, yes, that is the cause of the war," said old Antonio, gravely. "And now, brother, there is a tail to you," turning to the tall, gray-haired Felipe[1]; and clearing his throat, Felipe begins about the Coyote and the Bear.

1 Pronounced Fay-lée-peh.

V

THE COYOTE AND THE BEAR [1]

ONCE upon a time Ko-íd-deh (the Bear) and Too-wháy-deh (the Coyote) chanced to meet at a certain spot, and sat down to talk. After a while the Bear said:

"Friend Coyote, do you see what good land this is here? What do you say if we farm it together, sharing our labor and the crop?"

The Coyote thought well of it, and said so; and after talking, they agreed to plant potatoes in partnership.

"Now," said the Bear, "I think of a good way to divide the crop. I will take all that grows below the ground, and you take all that grows above it. Then each can take away his share when he is ready, and there will be no trouble to measure."

The Coyote agreed, and when the time came they plowed the place with a sharp stick and planted their potatoes. All summer they worked together in the field, hoeing down the weeds with stone hoes and letting in water now and then from the irrigating-ditch. When harvest-time came, the Coyote went and cut off all the potato-tops at the

---

[1] The Coyote, you must know, is very stupid about some things; and in almost all Pueblo fairy stories is the victim of one joke or another. The bear, on the other hand, is one of the wisest of animals.

ground and carried them home, and afterward the Bear scratched out the potatoes from the ground with his big claws and took them to his house. When the Coyote saw this his eyes were opened, and he said:

"But this is not fair. You have those round things, which are good to eat, but what I took home we cannot eat at all, neither my wife nor I."

"But, friend Coyote," answered the Bear, gravely, "did we not make an agreement? Then we must stick to it like men."

The Coyote could not answer, and went home; but he was not satisfied.

The next spring, as they met one day, the Bear said:

"Come, friend Coyote, I think we ought to plant this good land again, and this time let us plant it in corn. But last year you were dissatisfied with your share, so this year we will change. You take what is below the ground for your share, and I will take only what grows above."

This seemed very fair to the Coyote, and he agreed. They plowed and planted and tended the corn; and when it came harvest-time the Bear gathered all the stalks and ears and carried them home. When the Coyote came to dig his share, he found nothing but roots like threads, which were good for nothing. He was very much dissatisfied; but the Bear reminded him of their agreement, and he could say nothing.

That winter the Coyote was walking one day by the river (the Rio Grande), when he saw the Bear sitting on the ice and eating a fish. The Coyote was very fond of fish, and coming up, he said:

"Friend Bear, where did you get such a fat fish?"

"Oh, I broke a hole in the ice," said the Bear, "and fished for them. There are many here." And he went on eating, without offering any to the Coyote.

"Won't you show me how, friend?" asked the Coyote, fainting with hunger at the smell of the fish.

"Oh, yes," said the Bear. "It is very easy." And he broke a hole in the ice with his paw. "Now, friend Coyote, sit down and let your tail hang in the water, and very soon you will feel a nibble. But you must not pull it till I tell you."

So the Coyote sat down with his tail in the cold water. Soon the ice began to form around it, and he called:

"Friend Bear, I feel a bite! Let me pull him out."

"No, no! Not yet!" cried the Bear, "wait till he gets a good hold, and then you will not lose him."

So the Coyote waited. In a few minutes the hole was frozen solid, and his tail was fast.

"Now, friend Coyote," called the Bear, "I think you have him. Pull!"

The Coyote pulled with all his might, but could not lift his tail from the ice, and there he was — a prisoner. While he pulled and howled, the Bear shouted with laughter, and rolled on the ice and ha-ha'd till his sides were sore. Then he took his fish and went home, stopping every little to laugh at the thought of the Coyote.

There on the ice the Coyote had to stay until a thaw liberated him, and when he got home he was very wet and cold and half starved. And from that day to this he has never forgiven the Bear, and will not even speak to him when they meet, and the Bear says, politely, "Good morning, friend Too-wháy-deh."

"Is that so?" cry the boys.

"That is so," says Felipe. "But now it is time to go home. *Tóo-kwai!*"

The story-telling is over for to-night. Grandmother Reyes is unrolling the mattresses upon the floor; and with pleasant "good-nights" we scatter for our homes here and there in the quaint adobe village.

VI

"NOW there is a tail to you, *compadre* [friend]," said old Desiderio, nodding at Patricio[1] after we had sat awhile in silence around the crackling fire.

Patricio had a broad strip of rawhide across his knee, and was scraping the hair from it with a dull knife. It was high time to be thinking of new soles, for already there was a wee hole in the bottom of each of his moccasins; and as for Benito, his shy little grandson, *his* toes were all abroad.

But shrilly as the cold night-wind outside hinted the wisdom of speedy cobbling, Patricio had no wish

1 Pronounced Pah-trée-see-oh.

34

to acquire that burro's tail, so, laying the rawhide and knife upon the floor beside him, he deliberately rolled a modest pinch of the aromatic *koo-ah-rée* in a corn-husk, lighted it at the coals, and drew Benito's tousled head to his side.

"You have heard," he said, with a slow puff, "about Nah-chu-rú-chu, the mighty medicine-man who lived here in Isleta in the times of the ancients?"

"*A h-h!*" (Yes) cried all the boys. "You have promised to tell us how he married the moon!"

"Another time I will do so. But now I shall tell you something that was before that — for Nah-chu rú-chu had many strange adventures before he married Páh-hlee-oh, the Moon-Mother. Do you know why the rattlesnake— which is the king of all snakes and alone has the power of death in his mouth — always shakes his *guaje*[1] before he bites?"

"*Een-dah!*" chorused Ramón and Benito, and Fat Juan, and Tomás,[2] very eagerly; for they were particularly fond of hearing about the exploits of the greatest of Tée-wahn medicine-men.

"Listen, then, and you shall hear."

In those days Nah-chu-rú-chu had a friend who lived in a pueblo nearer the foot of the Eagle-Feather Mountain than this, in the Place of the Red Earth, where still are its ruins; and the two young men went often to the mountain together to bring wood and to hunt. Now, Nah-chu-rú-

---

[1] The Pueblo sacred rattle.
[2] Pronounced Rah-móhn, Bay-née-toh, Whahn, Toh-máhs.

chu had a white heart, and never thought ill; but the friend had the evil road and became jealous, for Nah-chu-rú-chu was a better hunter. But he said nothing, and made as if he still loved Nah-chu-rú-chu truly.

One day the friend came over from his village and said:

"Friend Nah-chu-rú-chu, let us go to-morrow for wood and to have a hunt.

"It is well," replied Nah-chu-rú-chu. Next morning he started very early and came to the village of his friend; and together they went to the mountain. When they had gathered much wood, and lashed it in bundles for carrying, they started off in opposite directions to hunt. In a short time each returned with a fine fat deer.

"But why should we hasten to go home, friend Nah-chu-rú-chu?" said the friend. "It is still early, and we have much time. Come, let us stop here and amuse ourselves with a game."

"It is well, friend," answered Nah-chu-rú-chu; "but what game shall we play? For we have neither *pa-toles*, nor hoops, nor any other game here."

"See! we will roll the *mah-khúr*,[1] for while I was waiting for you I made one that we might play"—and the false friend drew from beneath his blanket a pretty painted hoop; but really he had

---

[1] The game of *mah-khúr*, which the Pueblos learned from the Apaches many centuries ago, is a very simple one, but is a favorite with all witches as a snare for those whom they would injure. A small hoop of willow is painted gaily, and has ornamental buckskin thongs stretched across it from side to side, spoke-fashion. The challenger to a game rolls the hoop rapidly past the challenged, who must throw a lance through between the spokes before it ceases to roll.

"AS HE CAUGHT THE HOOP HE WAS INSTANTLY CHANGED INTO
A POOR COYOTE!"

made it at home, and had brought it hidden, on purpose to do harm to Nah-chu-rú-chu.

"Now go down there and catch it when I roll it," said he; and Nah-chu-rú-chu did so. But as he caught the hoop when it came rolling, he was no longer Nah-chu-rú-chu the brave hunter, but a poor Coyote with great tears rolling down his nose!

"Hu!" said the false friend, tauntingly, "we do this to each other! So now you have all the plains to wander over, to the north, and west, and south; but you can never go to the east. And if you are not lucky, the dogs will tear you; but if you are lucky, they may have pity on you. So now good-by, for this is the last I shall ever see of you."

Then the false friend went away, laughing, to his village; and the poor Coyote wandered aimlessly, weeping to think that he had been betrayed by the one he had loved and trusted as a brother. For four days he prowled about the outskirts of Isleta, looking wistfully at his home. The fierce dogs ran out to tear him; but when they came near they only sniffed at him, and went away without hurting him. He could find nothing to eat save dry bones, and old thongs or soles of moccasins.

On the fourth day he turned westward, and wandered until he came to Mesita.[1] There was no town of the Lagunas there then, and only a shepherd's hut and corral, in which were an old Quères Indian and his grandson, tending their goats.

Next morning when the grandson went out very early to let the goats from the corral, he saw a Coyote run out from among the goats. It went

---

[1] An outlying colony of Laguna, forty miles from Isleta.

off a little way, and then sat down and watched him. The boy counted the goats, and none were missing, and he thought it strange. But he said nothing to his grandfather.

For three more mornings the very same thing happened; and on the fourth morning the boy told his grandfather. The old man came out, and set the dogs after the Coyote, which was sitting a little way off; but when they came near they would not touch him.

"I suspect there is something wrong here," said the old shepherd; and he called: "Coyote, are you coyote-true, or are you people?"

But the Coyote could not answer; and the old man called again: "Coyote, are you people?"

At that the Coyote nodded his head, "Yes."

"If that is so, come here and be not afraid of us; for we will be the ones to help you out of this trouble."

So the Coyote came to them and licked their hands, and they gave it food — for it was dying of hunger. When it was fed, the old man said:

"Now, son, you are going out with the goats along the creek, and there you will see some willows. With your mind look at two willows, and mark them; and to-morrow morning you must go and bring one of them."

The boy went away tending the goats, and the Coyote stayed with the old man. Next morning, when they awoke very early, they saw all the earth wrapped in a white *manta*.[1]

---

[1] This figure is always used by the Pueblos in speaking of snow in connection with sacred things.

"COYOTE, ARE YOU PEOPLE?"

"Now, son," said the old man, "you must wear only your moccasins and breech-clout, and go like a man to the two willows you marked yesterday. To one of them you must pray; and then cut the other and bring it to me."

The boy did so and came back with the willow stick. The old man prayed, and made a *mah-khúr* hoop; and bidding the Coyote stand a little way off and stick his head through the hoop before it should stop rolling, rolled it toward him. The Coyote waited till the hoop came very close, and gave a great jump and put his head through it before it could stop. And lo! there stood Nah-chu-rú-chu, young and handsome as ever; but his beautiful suit of fringed buckskin was all in rags. For four days he stayed there and was cleansed with the cleansing of the medicine-man; and then the old shepherd said to him:

"Now, friend Nah-chu-rú-chu, there is a road.[1] But take with you this *faja*,[2] for though your power is great, you have submitted to this evil. When you get home, he who did this to you will be first to know, and he will come pretending to be your friend, as if he had done nothing; and he will ask you to go hunting again. So you must go; and when you come to the mountain, with this *faja* you shall repay him."

Nah-chu-rú-chu thanked the kind old shepherd, and started home. But when he came to the Bad Hill and looked down into the valley of the Rio Grande, his heart sank. All the grass and

---

[1] That is, you can go home.
[2] A fine woven belt, with figures in red and green.

fields and trees were dry and dead — for Nah-chu-rú-chu was the medicine-man who controlled the clouds, so no rain could fall when he was gone; and the eight days he had been a Coyote were in truth eight years. The river was dry, and the springs; and many of the people were dead from thirst, and the rest were dying. But as Nah-chu-rú-chu came down the hill, it began to rain again, and all the people were glad.

When he came into the pueblo, all the famishing people came out to welcome him. And soon came the false friend, making as if he had never bewitched him nor had known whither he disappeared.

In a few days the false friend came again to propose a hunt; and next morning they went to the mountain together. Nah-chu-rú-chu had the pretty *faja* wound around his waist; and when the wind blew his blanket aside, the other saw it.

"Ay! What a pretty *faja!*" cried the false friend. "Give it to me, friend Nah-chu-rú-chu."

"*Een-dah!*" (No) said Nah-chu-rú-chu. But the false friend begged so hard that at last he said:

"Then I will roll it to you; and if you can catch it before it unwinds, you may have it."

So he wound it up,[1] and holding by one end gave it a push so that it ran away from him, unrolling as it went. The false friend jumped for it, but it was unrolled before he caught it.

"*Een-dah!*" said Nah-chu-rú-chu, pulling it back. "If you do not care enough for it to be spryer than that, you cannot have it."

---

[1] Like a roll of tape.

"AS HE SEIZED IT HE WAS CHANGED FROM A TALL YOUNG
MAN INTO A GREAT RATTLESNAKE."

The false friend begged for another trial; so Nah-chu-rú-chu rolled it again. This time the false friend caught it before it was unrolled; and lo! instead of a tall young man, there lay a great rattlesnake with tears rolling from his lidless eyes!

"We, too, do this to each other!" said Nah-chu-rú-chu. He took from his medicine-pouch a pinch of the sacred meal and laid it on the snake's flat head for its food; and then a pinch of the corn-pollen to tame it.[1] And the snake ran out its red forked tongue, and licked them.

"Now," said Nah-chu-rú-chu, "this mountain and all rocky places shall be your home. But you can never again do to another harm, without warning, as you did to me. For see, there is a *guaje*[2] in your tail, and whenever you would do any one an injury, you must warn them before-hand with your rattle."

"And is that the reason why Ch'ah-rah-ráh-deh always rattles to give warning before he bites?" asked Fat Juan, who is now quite as often called Juan Biscocho (John Biscuit), since I photographed him one day crawling out of the big adobe bake-oven where he had been hiding.

"That is the very reason. Then Nah-chu-rú-chu left his false friend, from whom all the rattle-snakes are descended, and came back to his village. From that time all went well with Isleta, for Nah-chu-rú-chu was at home again to attend to the clouds. There was plenty of rain, and the river began to run again, and the springs flowed.

---

[1] This same spell is still used here by the *Hee-but-hái,* or snake-charmers.
[2] Pronounced Gwáh-heh.

The people plowed and planted again, as they had
not been able to do for several years, and all their
work prospered.   As for the people who lived in
the Place of the Red Earth, they all moved down
here,[1] because the Apaches were very bad ; and
here their descendants live to this day."

"Is that so?" sighed all the boys in chorus,
sorry that the story was so soon done.

"That is so," replied old Patricio.   "And now,
compadre Antonio, there is a tail to you."

"Well, then, I will tell a story which they
showed me in Taos[2] last year," said the old man.

"Ah-h!" said the boys.

"It is about the Coyote and the Woodpecker."

[1] It is a proved fact that there was such a migration.
[2] The most northern of the Pueblo cities.   Its people are also Tée-wahn.

VII

THE COYOTE AND THE WOODPECKER

WELL, once upon a time a Coyote and his family lived near the edge of a wood. There was a big hollow tree there, and in it lived an old Woodpecker and his wife and children. One day as the Coyote-father was strolling along the edge of the forest he met the Woodpecker-father.

"*Hin-no-kah-kée-ma*" (Good evening), said the Coyote; "how do you do to-day, friend Hloo-rée-deh?"

"Very well, thank you; and how are you, friend Too-wháy-deh?"

So they stopped and talked together awhile; and when they were about to go apart the Coyote said:

"Friend Woodpecker, why do you not come as friends to see us? Come to our house to supper this evening, and bring your family."

"Thank you, friend Coyote," said the Woodpecker; "we will come with joy."

So that evening, when the Coyote-mother had made supper ready, there came the Woodpecker-father and the Woodpecker-mother with their three children. When they had come in, all five of the Woodpeckers stretched themselves as they do after flying, and by that showed their pretty feathers — for the Hloo-ŕée-deh has yellow and red marks under its wings. While they were eating supper, too, they sometimes spread their

THE COYOTES AT SUPPER WITH THE WOODPECKERS.

wings, and displayed their bright under-side. They praised the supper highly, and said the Coyote-mother was a perfect housekeeper. When it was time to go, they thanked the Coyotes very kindly and invited them to come to supper at their house the following evening. But when they were gone, the Coyote-father could hold himself no longer, and he said:

"Did you see what airs those Woodpeckers put on? Always showing off their bright feathers? But I want them to know that the Coyotes are equal to them. *I 'll* show them!"

Next day, the Coyote-father had all his family at work bringing wood, and built a great fire in front of his house. When it was time to go to the house of the Woodpeckers he called his wife and children to the fire, and lashed a burning stick under each of their arms, with the burning end pointing forward; and then he fixed himself in the same way.

"Now," said he, "we will show them! When we get there, you must lift up your arms now and then, to show them that we are as good as the Woodpeckers."

When they came to the house of the Woodpeckers and went in, all the Coyotes kept lifting their arms often, to show the bright coals underneath. But as they sat down to supper, one Coyote-girl gave a shriek and said:

"Oh, *tata!* My fire is burning me!"

"Be patient, my daughter," said the Coyote-father, severely, "and do not cry about little things."

"Ow!" cried the other Coyote-girl in a moment, "my fire has gone out!"

This was more than the Coyote-father could stand, and he reproved her angrily.

"But how is it, friend Coyote," said the Woodpecker, politely, "that your colors are so bright at first, but very soon become black?"

"Oh, that is the beauty of our colors," replied the Coyote, smothering his rage; "that they are not always the same—like other people's—but turn all shades."

But the Coyotes were very uncomfortable, ana made an excuse to hurry home as soon as they could. When they got there, the Coyote-father whipped them all for exposing him to be laughed at. But the Woodpecker-father gathered his children around him, and said:

"Now, my children, you see what the Coyotes have done. Never in your life try to appear what you are not. Be just what you really are, and put on no false colors."

"Is that so?" cried the boys.

"That is so; and it is as true for people as for birds. Now, *tóo-kwai*—for it is bedtime."

VIII

MONG the principal heroes of the Tée-wahn folk-lore, I hear of none more frequently in the winter story-tellings to which my aboriginal neighbors admit me, than the mighty Nah-chu-rú-chu. To this day his name, which means "The Bluish Light of Dawn," is deeply revered by the quaint people who claim him as one of their forefathers. He had no parents, for he was created by the Trues themselves, and by them was given such extraordinary powers as were second only to their own. His wonderful

feats and startling adventures — as still related by
the believing Isleteños — would fill a volume. One
of these fanciful myths has interested me particularly, not only for its important bearing on certain
ethnological matters, but for its intrinsic qualities
as well. It is a thoroughly characteristic leaf from
the legendary lore of the Southwest.

Long before the first Spaniards came to New
Mexico (and *that* was three hundred and fifty
years ago) Isleta stood where it stands to-day
— on a lava ridge that defies the gnawing current
of the Rio Grande.[1]   In those far days, Nah-chu-
rú-chu dwelt in Isleta, and was a leader of his
people.   A weaver by trade,[2] his rude loom hung
from the dark rafters of his room; and in it he
wove the strong black *mantas* which are the dress
of Pueblo women to this day.

Besides being very wise in medicine, Nah-chu-
rú-chu was young, and tall, and strong, and handsome; and all the girls of the village thought it a
shame that he did not care to take a wife.   For
him the shyest dimples played, for him the whitest
teeth flashed out, as the owners passed him in the
plaza; but he had no eyes for them.   Then, in
the naïve custom of the Tée-wahn, bashful fingers
worked wondrous fringed shirts of buckskin, or
gay awl-sheaths, which found their way to his
house by unknown messengers — each as much as

---

[1] Bandelier has published a contrary opinion, to which I do not think he
would now cling.   The folk-lore and the very name of the town fully prove to
me that its site has not changed in historic times.

[2] In the ancient days, weaving was practised only by the men, among the
Pueblos.   This old usage is now reversed, and it is the women who weave,
except in the pueblos of Moqui.

to say, "She who made this is yours, if you will have her." But Nah-chu-rú-chu paid no more attention to the gifts than to the smiles, and just kept weaving and weaving—such *mantas* as were never seen in the land of the Tée-wahn before or since.

The most persistent of his admirers were two sisters who were called *Ee-eh-chóo-ri-ch'áhm-nin* — the Yellow-Corn-Maidens. They were both young and pretty, but they "had the evil road" — which is the Indian way of saying that they were possessed of a magic power which they always used for ill. When all the other girls gave up, discouraged at Nah-chu-rú-chu's indifference, the Yellow-Corn-Maidens kept coming day after day, trying to attract him. At last the matter became such a nuisance to Nah-chu-rú-chu that he hired the deep-voiced town-crier to go through all the streets and announce that in four days Nah-chu-rú-chu would choose a wife.

For dippers, to take water from the big earthen *tinajas*, the Tée-wahn used then, as they use to-day, queer little ladle-shaped *omates* made of a gourd; but Nah-chu-rú-chu, being a great medicine-man and very rich, had a dipper of pure pearl, shaped like the gourds, but wonderfully precious.

"On the fourth day," proclaimed the crier, "Nah-chu-rú-chu will hang his pearl *omate* at his door, where every girl who will may throw a handful of corn-meal at it. And she whose meal is so well ground that it sticks to the *omate*, she shall be the wife of Nah-chu-rú-chu!"

When this strange news came rolling down the still evening air, there was a great scampering of

little moccasined feet. The girls ran out from
hundreds of gray adobe houses to catch every
word; and when the crier had passed on, they ran
back into the store-rooms and began to ransack the
corn-bins for the biggest, evenest, and most perfect
ears.   Shelling the choicest, each took her few
handfuls of kernels to the sloping *metate*,[1] and

THE ISLETA GIRLS GRINDING CORN WITH THE "MANO"
ON THE "METATE."

with the *mano*, or hand-stone, scrubbed the grist
up and down, and up and down, till the hard corn
was a soft, blue meal.   All the next day, and
the next, and the next, they ground it over and
over again, until it grew finer than ever flour was
before; and every girl felt sure that her meal
would stick to the *omate* of the handsome young
weaver.   The Yellow-Corn-Maidens worked hardest of all ; day and night for four days they ground
and ground, with all the magic spells they knew.

1 The slab of lava which still serves as a hand-mill in Pueblo houses.

Now, in those far-off days the Moon had not gone up into the sky to live, but was a maiden of Shee-eh-whíb-bak.   And a very beautiful girl she was, though blind of one eye. She had long admired Nah-chu-rú-chu, but was always too maidenly to try to attract his attention as other girls had done; and at the time when the crier made his proclama-tion, she happened to be away at her father's ranch. It was only upon the fourth day that she returned to town, and in a few moments the girls were to go with their meal to test it upon the magic dipper.   The two Yellow-Corn-Maidens were just coming from their house as she passed, and told her of what was to be done. They were very confident of success, and told the Moon-girl only to pain her; and laughed derisively as she went running to her home.

THE MOON-MAIDEN.

By this time a long file of girls was coming to Nah-chu-rú-chu's house, outside whose door hung the pearl *omate*.   Each girl carried in her left hand a little jar of meal; and as they passed the door one by one, each took from the jar a handful and threw it against the magic dipper. But each time the meal dropped to the ground, and left the pure pearl undimmed and radiant as ever.

At last came the Yellow-Corn-Maidens, who had waited to watch the failure of the others. As they came where they could see Nah-chu-rú-chu sitting at his loom, they called: "Ah! Here we have the meal that will stick!" and each threw a handful at the *omate*. But it did not stick at all; and still from his seat Nah-chu-rú-chu could see, in that mirror-like surface, all that went on outside.

The Yellow-Corn-Maidens were very angry, and instead of passing on as the others had done, they stood there and kept throwing and throwing at the *omate*, which smiled back at them with undiminished luster.

Just then, last of all, came the Moon, with a single handful of meal which she had hastily ground. The two sisters were in a fine rage by this time, and mocked her, saying:

"Hoh! *P'áh-hlee-oh*,[1] you poor thing, we are very sorry for you! Here we have been grinding our meal four days and still it will not stick, and you we did not tell till to-day. How, then, can you ever hope to win Nah-chu-rú-chu? Pooh, you silly little thing!"

But the Moon paid no attention whatever to their taunts. Drawing back her little dimpled hand, she threw the meal gently against the pearl *omate*, and so fine was it ground that every tiniest bit of it clung to the polished shell, and not a particle fell to the ground.

_____

[1] Tée-wahn name of the moon; literally, "Water-Maiden."

THE YELLOW-CORN-MAIDENS THROWING MEAL AT THE PEARL. "OMATE."

When Nah-chu-rú-chu saw that, he rose up quickly from his loom and came and took the Moon by the hand, saying, "You are she who shall be my wife. You shall never want for anything, since I have very much." And he gave her many beautiful *mantas*, and cotton wraps, and fat boots of buckskin that wrap round and round, that she might dress as the wife of a rich chief. But the Yellow-Corn-Maidens, who had seen it all, went away vowing vengeance on the Moon.

Nah-chu-rú-chu and his sweet Moon-wife were very happy together. There was no other such housekeeper in all the pueblo as she, and no other hunter brought home so much buffalo-meat from the vast plains to the east, nor so many antelopes, and black-tailed deer, and jack-rabbits from the Manzanos as did Nah-chu-rú-chu. But he constantly was saying to her:

"Moon-wife, beware of the Yellow-Corn-Maidens, for they have the evil road and will try to do you harm, but you must always refuse to do whatever they propose." And always the young wife promised.

One day the Yellow-Corn-Maidens came to the house and said:

"Friend Nah-chu-rú-chu, we are going to the *llano*[1] to gather *amole*.[2] Will you not let your wife go with us?"

"Oh, yes, she may go," said Nah-chu-rú-chu; but taking her aside, he said, "Now be sure that you refuse whatever they may propose."

---

[1] Plain.
[2] The soapy root of the palmilla, used for washing.

The Moon promised, and started away with the Yellow-Corn-Maidens.

In those days there was only a thick forest of cottonwoods where are now the smiling vineyards, and gardens, and orchards of Isleta, and to reach the *llano* the three women had to go through this forest. In the very center of it they came to a deep *pozo* — a square well, with steps at one side leading down to the water's edge.

"Ay!" said the Yellow-Corn-Maidens, "how hot and thirsty is our walk!. Come, let us get a drink of water."

But the Moon, remembering her husband's words, said politely that she did not wish to drink. They urged in vain, but at last, looking down into the *pozo*, called:

"Oh, Moon-friend! Come and look in this still water, and see how pretty you are!"

The Moon, you must know, has always been just as fond of looking at herself in the water as she is to this very day, and forgetting Nah-chu-rú-chu's warning, she came to the brink, and looked down upon her fair reflection. But at that very moment, the two witch-sisters pushed her head foremost into the *pozo*, and drowned her; and then filled the well with earth, and went away as happy as wicked hearts can be.

Nah-chu-rú-chu began to look oftener from his loom to the door as the sun crept along the adobe floor, closer and closer to his seat; and when the shadows were very long, he sprang suddenly to his feet, and walked to the house of the Yellow-Corn-Maidens with long, strong strides.

"*Ee-eh-chóo-ri-ch'áhm-nin*," he said, very sternly, "where is my little wife?"

"Why, is n't she at home?" asked the wicked sisters as if in great surprise. "She got enough *amole* long before we did, and started home with it. We supposed she had come long ago."

"Ah," groaned Nah-chu-rú-chu within himself; "it is as I thought — they have done her ill." But without a word to them he turned on his heel and went away.

From that hour all went ill with Isleta, for Nah-chu-rú-chu held the well-being of all his people, even unto life and death. Paying no attention to what was going on about him, he sat motionless upon the very crosspiece of the *estufa* ladder — the highest point in all the town — with his head bowed upon his hands. There he sat for days, never speaking, never moving. The children that played along the streets looked up to the motionless figure, and ceased their boisterous play. The old men shook their heads gravely, and muttered: "We are in evil times, for Nah-chu-rú-chu is mourning, and will not be comforted. And there is no more rain, so that our crops are drying in the fields. What shall we do?"

At last all the councilors met together, and decided that there must be another effort made to find the lost wife. It was true that the great Nah-chu-rú-chu had searched for her in vain, and the people had helped him; but perhaps some one else might be more fortunate. So they took some of the sacred smoking-weed wrapped in a corn-husk and went to Shée-wid-deh, who has the sharpest eyes in all the world. Giving him the sacred gift they said:

"Eagle-friend, we see Nah-chu-rú-chu in great trouble, for he has lost his Moon-wife. Come, search for her, we pray you, if she be alive or dead."

So the Eagle took the offering, and smoked the smoke-prayer; and then he went winging upward into the very sky. Higher and higher he rose, in great upward circles, while his keen eyes noted every stick, and stone, and animal on the face of all the world. But with all his eyes, he could see nothing of the lost wife; and at last he came back sadly, and said:

"People-friends, I went up to where I could see the whole world, but I could not find her."

Then the people went with an offering to the Coyote, whose nose is sharpest in all the world; and besought him to try to find the Moon. The Coyote smoked the smoke-prayer, and started off with his nose to the ground, trying to find her tracks. He trotted all over the earth; but at last he too came back without finding what he sought.

Then the troubled people got the Badger to search, for he is best of all the beasts at digging— and he it was whom the Trues employed to dig the caves in which the people first dwelt when they came to this world. The Badger trotted and pawed, and dug everywhere, but he could not find the Moon; and he came home very sad.

Then they asked the Osprey, who can see farthest under water, and he sailed high above all the lakes and rivers in the world, till he could count the

THE GRIEF OF NAH-CHU-RÚ-CHU.

pebbles and the fish in them, but he too failed to discover the lost Moon.

By now the crops were dead and sere in the fields, and thirsty animals walked crying along the dry river. Scarcely could the people themselves dig deep enough to find so much water as would keep them alive. They were at a loss which way to turn; but at last they thought: We will go to P'ah-kú-ee-teh-áy-deh,[1] who can find the dead — for surely she is dead, or the others would have found her.

So they went to him and besought him. The Turkey-buzzard wept when he saw Nah-chu-rú-chu still sitting there upon the ladder, and said: "Truly it is sad for our great friend; but for me, I am afraid to go, since they who are more mighty than I have already failed; but I will try." And spreading his broad wings he went climbing up the spiral ladder of the sky. Higher he wheeled, and higher, till at last not even the Eagle could see him. Up and up, till the hot sun began to singe his head, and not even the Eagle had ever been so high. He cried with pain, but still he kept mounting — until he was so close to the sun that all the feathers were burned from his head and neck. But he could see nothing; and at last, frantic with the burning, he came wheeling downward. When he got back to the *estufa* where all the people were waiting, they saw that his head and neck had been burnt bare of feathers — and from that day to this the feathers would never grow out again.

"And did you see nothing?" they all asked, when they had bathed his burns.

---

[1] Turkey-buzzard; literally, "water-goose-grandfather."

"Nothing," he answered, "except that when I was half-way down I saw in the middle of yon cottonwood forest a little mound covered with all the beautiful flowers in the world."

"Oh!" cried Nah-chu-rú-chu, speaking for the first time. "Go, friend, and bring me one flower from the very middle of that mound."

Off flew the Buzzard, and in a few minutes returned with a little white flower. Nah-chu-rú-chu took it, and descending from the ladder in silence, walked to his house, while all the wondering people followed.

When Nah-chu-rú-chu came inside his home once more, he took a new *manta* and spread it in the middle of the room; and laying the wee white flower tenderly in its center, he put another new *manta* above it. Then, dressing himself in the splendid buckskin suit the lost wife had made him, and taking in his right hand the sacred *guaje* (rattle), he seated himself at the head of the *mantas* and sang:

> " *Shú-nah, shú-nah !*
> *A í-ay-ay, ai-ay-ay, ai-ay-ay !*"

> (Seeking her, seeking her !
> There-away, there-away !)

When he had finished the song, all could see that the flower had begun to grow, so that it lifted the upper *manta* a little. Again he sang, shaking his gourd; and still the flower kept growing. Again and again he sang; and when he had finished for the fourth time, it was plain to all that a human form lay between the two *mantas*. And

when he sang his song the fifth time, the form sat
up and moved.   Tenderly he lifted away the over-
cloth, and there sat his sweet Moon-wife, fairer than
ever, and alive as before! [1]

For four days the people danced and sang in the
public square.   Nah-chu-rú-chu was happy again;
and now the rain began to fall.   The choked earth
drank and was glad and green, and the dead crops
came to life.

When his wife told him how the witch-sisters
had done, he was very angry; and that very day
he made a beautiful hoop to play the *mah-khúr*.
He painted it, and put strings across it, decorated
with beaded buckskin.

"Now," said he, "the wicked Yellow-Corn-
Maidens will come to congratulate you, and will
pretend not to know where you were.   You must
not speak of that, but invite them to go out and
play a game with you."

In a day or two the witch-sisters did come, with
deceitful words; and the Moon invited them to go
out and play a game.   They went up to the edge
of the *llano*, and there she let them get a glimpse
of the pretty hoop.

"Oh, give us that, Moon-friend," they teased.
But she refused.   At last, however, she said:

"Well, we will play the hoop-game.   I will stand
here, and you there; and if, when I roll it to you,
you catch it before it falls upon its side, you may
have it."

1 Nah-chu-rú-chu's incantation followed the exact form still used by the
Indian conjurors of the Southwest in their wonderful trick of making corn
grow and mature from the kernel in one day.

So the witch-sisters stood a little way down the hill, and she rolled the bright hoop. As it came trundling to them, both grasped it at the same instant; and lo! instead of the Yellow-Corn-Maidens, there were two great snakes, with tears rolling down ugly faces. The Moon came and put upon their heads a little of the pollen of the corn-blossom (still used by Pueblo snake-charmers) to tame them, and a pinch of the sacred meal for their food.

"Now," said she, "you have the reward of treacherous friends. Here shall be your home among these rocks and cliffs forever, but you must never be found upon the prairie; and you must never bite a person. Remember you are women, and must be gentle."

And then the Moon went home to her husband, and they were very happy together. As for the sister snakes, they still dwell where she bade them, and never venture away; though sometimes the people bring them to their houses to catch the mice, for these snakes never hurt a person.

IX

AND do you know why it is that the Moon has but one eye? It is a short story, but one of the most poetic and beautiful in all the pretty folk-lore of the Pueblos.

P'áh-hlee-oh, the Moon-Maiden, was the Tée-wahn Eve[1]—the first and loveliest woman in all the world. She had neither father nor mother, sister nor brother; and in her fair form were the seeds of all humanity—of all life and love and goodness. The Trues, who are the unseen spirits that are above all, made T'hoor-íd-deh, the Sun, who was to be father of all things; and because he was alone, they made for him a companion, the first to be of maids, the first to be a wife. From them began the world and all that is in it; and all their children were strong and good. Very happy were the Father-all and the Mother-all, as they watched their happy brood. He guarded them by day and

---

[1] She is honored in almost every detail of the Pueblo ceremonials. The most important charm or implement of the medicine-men, the holiest fetish of all, is typical of her. It is called Mah-pah-róo, the Mother, and is the most beautiful article a Pueblo ever fashioned. A flawless ear of pure white corn (a type of fertility or motherhood) is tricked out with a downy mass of snow-white feathers, and hung with ornaments of silver, coral, and the precious turquoise.

she by night—only there *was* no night, for then the Moon had two eyes, and saw as clearly as the Sun, and with glance as bright. It was all as one long day of golden light. The birds flew always, the flowers never shut, the young people danced and sang, and none knew how to rest.

But at last the Trues thought better. For the endless light grew heavy to the world's young eyes that knew no tender lids of night. And the Trues said:

"It is not well, for so there is no sleep, and the world is very tired. We must not keep the Sun and Moon seeing alike. Let us put out one of his eyes, that there may be darkness for half the time, and then his children can rest." And they called T'hoor-íd-deh and P'áh-hlee-oh before them to say what must be done.

But when she heard that, the Moon-Mother wept for her strong and handsome husband, and cried:

"No! No! Take my eyes, for my children, but do not blind the Sun! He is the father, the provider — and how shall he watch against harm, or how find us game without his bright eyes? Blind me, and keep him all-seeing."

And the Trues said: "It is well, daughter." And so they took away one of her eyes, so that she could never see again so well. Then night came upon the tired earth, and the flowers and birds and people slept their first sleep, and it was very good. But she who first had the love of children, and paid for them with pain as mother's pay, she did not grow ugly by her sacrifice. Nay, she is lovelier than ever, and we all love her to this day. For the Trues are good to her, and gave her in place of the bloom of girlhood the beauty that is only in the faces of mothers.

So mother-pale above us
   She bends, her watch to keep,
Who of her sight dear-bought the night
   To give her children sleep.

X

YOU have perhaps seen the beautiful arrow-heads of moss-agate, petrified wood, or volcanic glass which were used, until very recently, by the Indians of the Southwest, and are still treasured by them. At least you are familiar with the commoner flint ones left by the aboriginal tribes farther eastward. And seeing them, you must have wondered how they were ever made from such fearfully stubborn stone — always the very hardest that was accessible to the maker. I have tried for six hours, with the finest drills, to make a little hole in the thinnest part of an agate arrow-head, to put it on a charm-ring; but when the drill and I were completely worn out, there was not so much as a mark on the arrow-head to show what we had been doing. If you will take one to your jeweler, he will have as poor luck.

But the *making* of the arrow-heads is really a very simple matter; and I have fashioned many very fair ones. The only implements are part of a peculiarly shaped bone — preferably from the thigh of the elk — and a stick about the size of a lead-pencil, but of double the diameter. The maker of *puntas* takes the bone in his left hand; in his right is the stick, against which the selected splinter of stone is firmly pressed by the thumb.   With a firm, steady pressure against the sharp edge of the bone, a tiny flake is nicked from the splinter. Then the splinter is turned, and a nick is similarly made on the other side, just a little ahead of the first; and so on.   It is by this alternate nicking from opposite sides that the stone-splinter grows less by tiny flakes, and is shaped by degrees to a perfect arrow-head. If you will notice the edge of an arrow-head, you will see plainly that the work was done in this way, for the edge is not a straight but a wavy line — sometimes even a zigzag, recalling the manner in which saw-teeth are "set."

Every Indian, and every one who has studied the Indian, knows this.   But if I ask one of my brown old *compadres* here, where he got the arrow-head which he wears as a charm about his wrinkled neck, he will not tell me any such story as that.   No, indeed!

Quáh-le-kee-raí-deh, the Horned Toad, gave it to him. So? Oh, yes! He talked so nicely to a Horned Toad on the mesa [1] the other day, that the little creature put a *punta* where he could find it the next time he went thither.

Whenever a Pueblo sees a Quáh-le-kee-raí-deh, he jumps from his horse or his big farm-wagon, and makes every effort to capture the *animalito* before it can reach a hole. If successful, he pulls from his blanket or his legging-garters a red thread — no other color will do — and ties it necklace-fashion

1 Table-land.

around the neck of his little prisoner. Then he invokes all sorts of blessings on the Horned Toad, assures it of his sincere respect and friendship, begs it to remember him with a *punta*, and lets it go. Next time he goes to the mesa, he fully expects to find an arrow-head, and generally *does* find one—doubtless because he then searches more carefully on that broad reach where so many arrow-heads have been lost in ancient wars and hunts. Finding one, he prays to the Sun-Father and the Moon-Mother and all his other deities, and returns profound thanks to the Horned Toad. Some finders put the arrow-head in the pouch which serves Indians for a pocket.[1] Some wear it as an amulet on the necklace. In either case, the belief is that no evil spirit can approach the wearer while he has that charm about him. In fact, it is a sovereign spell against witches.

The common belief of the Pueblos is that the Horned Toad makes these arrow-heads only during a storm, and deposits them at the very instant when it thunders. For this reason an arrow-head is always called *Kóh-un-shée-eh*, or thunder-knife. The strange appearance of this quaint, spiked lizard — which is really not a "hop-toad" at all—doubtless suggested the notion ; for his whole back is covered with peculiar points which have very much the shape and color of Indian arrow-heads.

Quáh-le-kee-raí-deh is a very important personage in the Pueblo folk-lore. He not only is the inventor and patentee of the arrow-head and the

---

[1] The "left-hand-bag," *shur-taí-moo*, because it always hangs from the right shoulder and under the left arm.

scalping-knife,[1] but he also invented irrigation, and taught it to man; and is a general benefactor of our race.

There is one very sacred folk-story which tells why boys must never smoke until they have proved their manhood. Pueblo etiquette is very strict on all such points.[2]

Once upon a time there lived in Isleta two boys who were cousins. One day their grandfather, who was a True Believer (in all the ancient rites), caught them in a corner smoking the *weer*. Greatly shocked, he said to them:

"Sons, I see you want to be men; but you must prove yourselves before you are thought to be. Know, then, that nobody is born with the freedom of the smoke, but every one must earn it. So go now, each of you, and bring me Quée-hla-kú-ee, the skin of the oak."

Now, in the talk of men, Quée-hla-kú-ee is another thing; but the boys did not know. They got their mothers to give them some tortillas,[3] and with this lunch they started for the Bosque (a 10,000-foot peak twenty miles east of Isleta). Reaching the mountain, they went to every kind of tree and cut a little piece of its bark — for they were not sure which was the oak. Then they came home, very tired, and carried the bark to their grandfather. But when he had looked at it all he said:

[1] Which were formerly about the same thing — a large and sharp-edged arrow-head or similar stone being the only knife of the Pueblos in prehistoric times.

[2] See my "Strange Corners of Our Country" (The Century Co.), chap. xviii.

[3] A cake of unleavened batter cooked on a hot stone. They look something like a huge flapjack, but are very tough and keep a long time.

"Young men, you have not yet proved your-selves. So now it is for you to go again and look for the *oak*-bark."

At this their hearts were heavy, but they took tortillas and started again. On the way they met an old Horned Toad, who stopped them and said:

"Young-men-friends, I know what trouble you are in. Your *tata* has sent you for the skin of the oak, but you do not know the oak he means. But I will be the one to help you. Take these," and he gave them two large thunder-knives, "and with these in hand go up that cañon yonder. In a little way you will see a great many of your enemies, the Navajos, camping. On the first hill from which you see their fire, there stop. In time, while you wait there, you will hear a Coyote howling across the cañon. Then is the time to give your enemy-yell [war-whoop] and attack them."

The boys thanked the Horned Toad and went. Presently they saw the camp-fire of the Navajos, and waiting till the Coyote called they gave the enemy-yell and then attacked. They had no weap-ons except their thunder-knives, but with these they killed several Navajos, and the others ran away. In the dark and their hurry they made a mistake and scalped a woman (which was never customary with the Pueblos).

Taking their scalps, they hurried home to their grandfather, and when he saw that they had brought the real oak-skin (which is an Indian euphemy for "scalp"), he led them proudly to the Cacique, and the Cacique ordered the T'u-a-fú-ar (scalp-dance). After the inside days, when the

takers of scalps must stay in the *estufa*, was the
dance.   And when it came to the round dance at
night the two boys were dancing side by side.

Then a young woman who was a stanger came
and pushed them apart and danced between them.
She was very handsome, and both fell in love with
her.   But as soon as their hearts thought of love,
a skeleton was between them in place of the girl
— for they who go to war or take a scalp have no
right to think of love.

They were very frightened, but kept dancing until they were too tired, and then went to the singers
inside the circle to escape.   But the skeleton followed them and stood beside them, and they could
not hide from it.

At last they began to run away, and went to the
east.   Many moons they kept running, but the
skeleton was always at their heels.   At last they
came to the Sunrise Lake, wherein dwell the Trues
of the East.

The guards let them in, and they told the Trues
all that had happened, and the skeleton stood beside them.   The Trues said: "Young men, if you
are men, sit down and we will protect you."

But when the boys looked again at the skeleton
they could not stop, but ran away again.   Many
moons they ran north till they came to where the
Trues of the North dwell in the Black Lake of
Tears.

The Trues of the North promised to defend
them, but again the skeleton came and scared
them away; and they ran for many moons until
they came to the Trues of the West, who dwell

in T'hoor-kím-p'ah-whée-ay, the Yellow Lake
Where the Sun Sets. And there the same things
happened; and they ran away again to the south,
till they found the Trues of the South in P'ah-chéer-
p'ah-whée-ay, the Lake of Smooth Pebbles.

But there again it was the same, and again they
ran many moons till they came to the Trues of the
Center, who live here in Isleta. And here the
skeleton said to them:

"Why do you run from me now? For when
you were dancing you looked at me and loved me,
but now you run away."

But they could not answer her, and ran into the
room of the Trues of the Center, and told their
story. Then the Trues gave power to the Cum-
pa-huit-la-wid-deh[1] to see the skeleton,—which
no one else in the world could see, except the
Trues and the two young men,—and said to him:

"Shoot this person who follows these two."

So the Cum-pa-huit-la-wid-deh shot the skeleton through with an arrow from the left side to the
right side,[2] and took the scalp.

That was the end of the skeleton, and the young
men were free. And when the Trues had given
them counsel, they came to their people, and told
the Cacique all. He made a new scalp-dance, because they had not stayed to finish the first one.

And when the dance was done, they told all the
people what had happened. Then the principals
had a meeting and made a rule which is to this

---

[1] Guard at the door of the gods.
[2] The only official method of killing a witch, which is one of the chief
duties of the Cum-pa-huit-la-wen.

day, that in the twelve days of the scalp[1] no warrior shall think thoughts of love.

For it was because they had love-thoughts of
the Navajo girl that her skeleton haunted them.
And at the same time it was made the law, which
still is, that no one shall smoke till he has taken a
scalp to prove himself a man.

For if the boys had not been smoking when
they had not freedom to, their grandfather would
not have sent them, and all that trouble would not
have come.   And that is why.

[1] The period of fasting and purification before and during the scalp-
dance.

XI

THE Horned Toad is also a famous musician—
a sort of Pueblo Orpheus, whose song charms
the very stones and trees. A short folk-story of
Isleta refers to this.

One day Quáh-le-kee-raí-deh was working in
his field. There were many very large rocks,
and to move them he sang a strong song as he
pulled:

> *Yah éh-ah, héh-ah háy-na,*
> *Yah, éh-ah, heh-ah hay-na,*
> *Wha-naí-kee-ay hee-e-wid-deh*
> *Ah-kwe-ée-hee ai-yén-cheh,*
> *Yahb-k'yáy-queer ah-chóo-hee.*

When he sang this and touched the heaviest stone,
it rose up from the ground, and went over his head
and fell far behind him.

While he worked so, Too-wháy-deh came along;
and seeing what happened, he wished to meddle,
as his way is. So he said:

"Friend Quáh-le-kee-raí-deh, let *me* do it."

"No, friend," said the Horned Toad. "It is
better for every one to do what he knows, and not
to put himself in the work of others."

"Do not think so," answered the Coyote. "For I can do this also. It is very easy."

"It is well, then — but see that you are not afraid; for so it will be bad."

Too-wháy-deh laid off his blanket and took hold of the largest rock there was, and sang the song. When he sang, the rock rose up in the air to go over his head; but he, being scared, ducked his head. Then at once the rock fell on him, and he had no bones left. Then the Horned Toad laughed, and gave the enemy-yell (war-whoop), saying: "We do this to one another!"

XII

ANOTHER Isleta myth tells of an equally sad misadventure of the Coyote.

Once upon a time an old Coyote-father took a walk away from home; for in that season of the year his babies were so peevish they would not let him sleep. It happened that a Locust was making pottery, under a tree; and every time she moved the molding-spoon around the soft clay jar, she sang a song. The Coyote, coming near and hearing, thought: "Now that is the very song I need to put my *óo-un* to sleep." And following the sound he came to the tree, and found Cheech-wée-deh at work. But she had stopped singing.

"Locust-friend," said he, "come teach me that song, so that I can soothe my children to sleep." But the Locust did not move to answer; and he repeated:

"Locust-friend, come teach me that song."

Still she did not answer, and the Coyote, losing his patience, said:

"Locust, if you don't teach me that song, I will eat you up!"

At that, the Locust showed him the song, and he sang with her until he knew how.

"Now I know it, thank you," he said. "So I will go home and sing it to my children, and they will sleep."

So he went. But as he came to a pool, half-way home, a flock of Afraids-of-the-Water[1] flew up at his very nose, and drove out his memory. He went looking around, turning over the stones and peeping in the grass; but he could not find the song anywhere. So he started back at last to get the Locust to teach him again.

But while he was yet far, the Locust saw him, so she shed her skin, leaving a dry husk, as snakes do, and filled it with sand. Then she made it to sit up, and put the molding-spoon in its hands, and the clay jars in front of it; and she herself flew up into the tree.

Coming, the Coyote said: "Friend Locust, show that song again; for I got scared, and the song was driven out of me." But there was no answer.

"Hear, Locust! I will ask just once more; and if you do not show me the song, I 'll swallow you!"

Still she did not reply; and the Coyote, being angry, swallowed the stuffed skin, sand, spoon, and all, and started homeward, saying: "*Now* I think I have that song in me!"

But when he was half-way home he stopped and struck himself, and said: "What a fool, truly! For now I am going home without a song. But if I had left the Locust alive, and bothered her long enough, she would have shown me. I think now

1 The ironical Tée-wahn name for ducks.

8

I will take her out, to see if she will not sing for me."

So he ran all around, hunting for a black thunder-knife,[1] and singing:

> Where can I find Shée-eh-fóon ?
> Where can I find Shée-eh-fóon ?

At last he found a large piece of the black-rock, and broke it until he got a knife. He made a mark on his breast with his finger, saying: " Here I will cut, and take her out."

Then he cut. "Mercy!" said he, "but it bites!" He cut again, harder. "Goodness! but how it bites!" he cried, very loud. And cutting a third time, he fell down and died. So he did not learn the song of the pottery-making.

The Quères Pueblos have exactly the same folk-story, except that they make the Horned Toad, instead of the Locust, the music-teacher. In their version, the Horned Toad, after being swallowed, kills the Coyote by lifting its spines. Remembering what I have said of the maker of the thunder-knives, you will readily see the analogy between this and the obsidian splinter of the Tée-wahn story. It is, indeed, one of the most characteristic and instructive examples of the manner in which a folk-story becomes changed.

---

[1] One of obsidian, or volcanic glass.

XIII

FANCY I must have been dozing after that hard ride; for when a far-away, cracked voice that could be none other than Grandfather Ysidro's said, *"Kah-whee-cá-me, Lorenso-kai-deh!"* I started up so hastily as to bump my head against the whitewashed wall. That may seem a queer sentence to rouse one so sharply; and especially when you know what it means. It meant that old Ysidro[1] had just finished a story, which I had altogether missed, and was now calling upon the old man next him to tell one, by using the customary Pueblo saying:

"There is a tail to you, Father Lorenso!"

[1] Pronounced Ee-seé-droh.

Kah-whee-cá-me is what a Tée-wahn Indian always says in such a case, instead of "Now *you* tell
a story, friend." It is not intended as an impolite
remark, but merely refers to the firm belief of these
quaint people that if one were to act like a stubborn donkey, and refuse to tell a story when called
on, a donkey's tail would grow upon him!

With such a fate in prospect, you may be sure
that the roundabout invitation thus conveyed is
never declined.

Grandfather Lorenso bows his head gravely,
but seems in no haste. He is indeed impressively
deliberate as he slowly makes a cigarette from a
bit of corn-husk and a pinch of tobacco, lights it
upon a coal raked out of the fireplace by his
withered fingers, blows a slow puff eastward, then
one to the north, another to the west, a fourth to
the south, one straight above his head, and one
down toward the floor. There is one part of the
United States where the compass has *six* cardinal
points (those I have just named), and that is among
these Indians, and in fact all the others of the
Southwest. The cigarette plays a really important part in many sacred ceremonies of the
Pueblos; for, as I have explained, its collective
smoke is thought to be what makes the rain-
clouds and brings the rain; and it is also a charm
against witches.

Having thus propitiated the divinities who dwell
in the directions named, Lorenso looks about the
circle to see if all are listening. The glance satis-
fies him — as well it may. There are no heedless
eyes or ears in the audience, of which I am the

only white member — and a very lucky one, in
that I, an "Americano," am allowed to hear these
jealously guarded stories, and to see the silent
smoke-prayer which would never be made if a
stranger were present. There are seven agèd
men here, and nine bright-eyed boys — all *Isleteños* (inhabitants of Isleta). We are huddled
around the fireplace in the corner of the big,
pleasant room, against whose dark rafters and
farther white walls the shadows dance and waver.

And now, taking a deep puff, Lorenso exclaims:
"*Nah-t' hóo-ai!*" (In a house.) It has nothing
to do with the story; but is the prologue to in-
form the hearers that the story is about to open.

"Ah-h-h!" we all responded, which is as much
as to say, "We are listening—go on"; and Lorenso
begins his story.

Once upon a time there was a Tée-wahn village
on the other side of the mountain, and there lived
a man and his wife who thought more of the future
of their children than did the others. To care
better for the children they moved to a little ranch
some distance from the village, and there taught
their two little sons all they could. Both boys
loved the outdoors, and games, and hunting; and
the parents were well pleased, saying to each
other:

"Perhaps some day they will be great hunters!"

By the time the elder boy was twelve and the
younger ten, they both were very expert with the
little bows and arrows their father carefully made
them; and already they began to bring home many

rabbits when they were allowed to go a little way
from home. There was only one command their
parents gave about their hunts; and that was that
they must never, never go south. They could
hunt to the east, north, and west, but not south.

Day after day they went hunting, and more
and more rabbits they killed, growing always more
expert.

One day when they had hunted eastward, the
elder boy said:

"Brother, can you say any reason why we must
not go south?"

"I know nothing," replied the younger, "except
what I overheard our parents saying one day.
They spoke of an old woman who lives in the
south who eats children; and for that they said
they would never let us go south."

"Pooh!" said the elder, "I think nothing of *that*.
The real reason must be that they wish to save the
rabbits in the south, and are afraid we would kill
them all. There must be many rabbits in that
bosque [forest] away down there. Let's go and
see — *they* won't know!"

The younger boy being persuaded, they started
off together, and after a long walk came to the
bosque. It was full of rabbits, and they were
having great sport, when suddenly they heard a
motherly voice calling through the woods. In a
moment they saw an old woman coming from the
south, who said to the boys:

"*Mah-kóo-oon* [grandchildren], what are you
doing here, where no one ever thinks to come?"

"We are hunting, Grandmother," they replied.
"Our parents would never let us come south; but

to-day we came to see if the rabbits are more numerous here than above."

"Oh!" said the old woman, "this game you see here is *nothing*. Come, and I will show you where there is much, and you can carry very large rabbits home to your parents." But she was deceiving them.

She had a big basket upon her back, and stooping for the boys to get into it, she carried them farther and farther into the woods. At last they came to an old, battered house; and setting the basket down, she said:

"Now we have come all the way here, where no one ever came before, and there is no way out. You can find no trail, and you will have to stay here contented, or I will eat you up!"

The boys were much afraid, and said they would stay and be contented. But the old woman went into the house and told her husband—who was as wicked as she—to get wood and build a big fire in the *horno*.[1] All day long the fire burned, and the oven became hotter than it had ever been. In the evening the old witch-woman raked out the coals, and calling the boys seized them and forced them into the fiery oven.

"*Tahb-kóon-nahm?*" (Is that so?) we all exclaimed—that being the proper response whenever the narrator pauses a moment.

"That is so," replied Lorenso, and went on.

Then the old woman put a flat rock over the little door of the oven, and another over the smoke-

---

[1] An outdoor bake-oven, made of clay, and shaped like a beehive.

hole, and sealed them both tight with clay. All that night she and her husband were chuckling to think what a nice breakfast they would have—for both of them were witch-people, and ate all the children they could find.

But in the morning when she unsealed the oven, there were the two boys, laughing and playing together 'unhurt — for the Wháy-nin [1] had come to their aid and protected them from the heat.

Leaving the boys to crawl out, the old woman ran to the house and scolded the old man terribly for not having made the oven hot enough. "Go this minute," she said, "and put in the oven all the wood that it will hold, and keep it burning all day!"

When night came, the old woman cleaned the oven, which was twice as hot as before; and again she put in the boys and sealed it up. But the next morning the boys were unhurt and went to playing.

The witch-woman was very angry then; and giving the boys their bows and arrows, told them to go and play. She stayed at home and abused the old witch-man all day for a poor fire-maker.

When the boys returned in the evening, she said:

"To-morrow, grandchildren, we will play *Nah-oo-p'ah-chée* (hide-and-seek), and the one who is found three times by the other shall pay his life."

The boys agreed,[2] and secretly prayed to the Trues to help them—for by this time they knew that the old man and the old woman "had the bad road."

[1] "The Trues," as the Pueblos call their highest divinities.
[2] For such a challenge, which was once a common one with the Indians, could not possibly be declined.

The next day came; and very soon the old woman called them to begin the game. The boys were to hide first; and when the old woman had turned her eyes and vowed not to look, they went to the door and hid, one against each of its jambs. There you could look and look, and see the wood through them—for the Trues, to help them, made them invisible. When they were safely hidden they whooped, "*Hee-táh!*" and the old woman began to hunt, singing the hide-and-seek song:

Hee-táh yahn
Hee choo-ah-kóo
Mee, mee, mee ?

(Now, now,
Which way
Went they, went they, went they?)

After hunting some time she called:

"You little fellows are on the door-posts. Come out!"

So the boys came out and "made blind" (covered their eyes) while the old woman went to hide. There was a pond close by, with many ducks on it; and making herself very little, she went and hid under the left wing of the duck with a blue head.[1]

When they heard her "*Hee-táh!*" the boys went searching and singing; and at last the elder cried out:

" Old woman, you are under the left wing of the whitest duck on the lake — the one with the blue head. Come out!"

This time the boys made themselves small and crawled into the quivers beside their bows and arrows. The old woman had to sing her song over a great many times, as she went hunting all around; but at last she called:

" Come out of the quivers where you are! "

Then the witch made herself very small indeed, and went behind the foot of a big crane that was standing on one leg near the lake. But at last the boys found her even there.

It was their last turn now, and the old woman felt very triumphant as she waited for them to hide. But this time they went up and hid themselves under the right arm of the Sun.[2] The old witch hunted everywhere, and used all her bad power, but in vain; and when she was tired out she had

---

[1] I should tell you that, being a witch, she could not possibly have gone under the right wing. Everything that is to the left belongs to the witches.

[2] Who is, in the Pueblo belief, the father of all things.

"THE WITCH MADE HERSELF VERY SMALL, AND WENT
BEHIND THE FOOT OF A BIG CRANE."

to cry, "*Hee-táh-ow!*" And then the boys came down from under the Sun's arm rejoicing.

The old witch, taking her last turn, went to the lake and entered into a fish, thinking that there she would be perfectly safe from discovery. It did take the boys a great while to find her; but at last they shouted:

"Old woman, you are in the biggest fish in the lake. Come out!"

As she came walking toward them in her natural shape again, they called: "Remember the agreement!" and with their sharp arrows they killed the old witch-woman and then the old witch-man. Then they took away the two wicked old hearts, and put in place of each a kernel of spotless corn; so that if the witches should ever come to life again they would no longer be witches, but people with pure, good hearts. They never did come to life, however, which was just as well.

Taking their bows and arrows, the boys — now young men, for the four "days" they had been with the witches were really four years — returned home. At the village they found their anxious parents, who had come to ask the Cacique to order all the people out to search.

When all saw the boys and heard their story, there was great rejoicing, for those two witch-people had been terrors to the village for years. On their account no one had dared go hunting to the south. And to this day the game is thicker there than anywhere else in the country, because it has not been hunted there for so long as in other places. The two young men were forgiven for disobedience

9

(which is a very serious thing at any age, among
the Pueblos), and were made heroes. The Cacique
gave them his two daughters for wives, and all
the people did them honor.[1]

" Is that so?" we responded; and Lorenso replied, " That is so," gathering his blanket and rising
to go without " putting a tail" to any one, for it
was already late.

I may add that the game of hide-and-seek is still
played by my dusky little neighbors, the Pueblo
children, and the searching-song is still sung by
them, exactly as the boys and the old witch played
and sang — but of course without their magical
talent at hiding.

---

[1] This story seems to be one of the myths about the Hero Twin Brothers,
the children of the Sun. They are, next to Sun-Father and Moon-Mother,
the chief deities of all the southwestern tribes. In the Quères folk-lore they
figure very prominently; but in the Tée-wahn are more disguised.

XIV

NEARLY every people has its own version of the race of the Hare and the Tortoise. That current among the Pueblos makes the Rabbit the hero, by a trick rather cleverer than Æsop's.

Once the Coyote came where Pee-oo-ée-deh, the little "cotton-tail" rabbit, sat at the door of his house, thinking.

"What do you think, friend Pee-oo-ée-deh?" said the Coyote.

"I am thinking, friend Too-wháy-deh, why some have large tails like you; but we have no tails. Perhaps if we had tails like yours, we could run straight; but now we have to hop."

"It is true, *ah-bóo*,"[1] said the Coyote, not knowing that the Rabbit laughed in his heart. "For I can run faster than any one, and never did any gain from me in the foot-races. But *you*,—you just hop like a bird."

The Rabbit made a sad face, and the Coyote said: "But come, friend Pee-oo-ée-deh, let us run a race. We will run around the world, and see

[1] Poor thing.

who will win. And whichever shall come in first, he shall kill the other and eat him."[1]

"It is well," answered the Rabbit. "In four days we will run."

Then the Coyote went home very glad. But Pee-oo-ée-deh called a *junta* of all his tribe, and told them how it was, and the way he thought to win the race. And when they had heard, they all said: "It is well. Fear not, for we will be the ones that will help you."

When the fourth day came, the Coyote arrived smiling, and threw down his blanket, and stood ready in only the dark blue *taparabo*,[2] saying: "But what is the use to run? For I shall win. It is better that I eat you now, before you are tired."

But the Rabbit threw off his blanket, and tightened his *taparabo*, and said: "Pooh! For the end of the race is far away, and *there* is time to talk of eating. Come, we will run around the four sides of the world.[3] But *I* shall run underground, for so it is easier for me."

Then they stood up side by side. And when they were ready, the Capitan shouted "*Hai-koo!*" and they ran. The Coyote ran with all his legs; but the Rabbit jumped into his hole and threw out sand, as those who dig very fast.

Now for many days the Coyote kept running to the east, and saw nothing of Pee-oo-ée-deh. But

---

[1] A challenge of this sort, with life as the stake, was very common among all Indians; and it was impossible for the challenged to decline. This story recalls that of the Antelope Boy. Four days always elapsed between the challenge and the race.

[2] Breech-clout, which is the only thing worn in a foot-race.

[3] Which the Pueblos believe to be flat and square.

just as he came to the east and was turning to the
north, up jumped a rabbit from under the ground
in front of him, and shouted: "We do this to one
another"; and jumped back in the hole and began
to throw out dirt very hard.

"Ai!" said the Coyote. "I wish I could run
under the ground like that, for it seems very easy.
For all these days I have run faster than ever any
one ran; yet Pee-oo-ée-deh comes to the east
ahead of me." But he did not know it was the
brother of Pee-oo-ée-deh, who had come out to
the east to wait for him.

So Too-wháy-deh ran harder; and after many
days he came to the end of the world, to the
north. But just as he was to turn west, up
sprang a rabbit in front of him, and taunted him,
and went back in its hole, digging.

The Coyote's heart was heavy, but he ran *very*
hard. "Surely," he said, "no one can run so fast
as *this*."

But when he came to the west, a rabbit sprang
up ahead of him, and mocked him, and went again
under the ground. And when he had run to the
south, there was the same thing. At last, very
tired and with his tongue out, he came in sight of
the starting-point, and there was Pee-oo-ée-deh,
sitting at the door of his house, smoothing his hair.
And he said: "Pooh! Coyote-friend, we do this to
one another. For now it is clear that big tails are
not good to run with, since I have been waiting
here a long time for you. Come here, then, that I
may eat you, though you are tough."

But Too-wháy-deh, being a coward, ran away and

would not pay his bet. And all the brothers of Pee-oo-ée-deh laughed for the trick they had put upon the Coyote.

In a case which I knew of, years ago, this folk-story seems to have given a hint to human racers. A Mexican who owned a large and very fleet-footed burro, challenged a young Indian of Acoma to a ten-mile race. The Indian was a very famous runner, and the challenger depended on the distance alone to wear him out. In accordance with the conditions the rivals started together from the goal, the Indian on foot, the Mexican on his burro. For about four miles the Indian left the galloping donkey far behind; but he could not keep up such a tremendous pace, and the burro began to gain. About midway of the course where the trail touches a great lava-flow, the Indian dove into a cave. Just as the Mexican was passing, out came an Indian, passed the burro with a magnificent spurt, and after a long run reached the farther goal about a hundred feet ahead. Unfortunately for him, however, the trick was detected — he was the twin brother of the challenged man, and had awaited him in the cave, taking up the race fresh when the first runner was tired!

XV

NEARLY all of you have seen pictures of the
Burro, the quaint little donkey of the Southwest. He is very small,— not more than half the
weight of a smallish mule,— but very strong, very
sure-footed, and very reliable. And he is one of
the drollest, "cutest," wisest-looking creatures on
earth.

T'ah-hlá-a-hloon, or Big-ears, as the Tée-wahn
call him, does not appear very often in their folk-
lore — and for a very natural reason. Most of
these myths were made centuries before a white
man ever saw this country; and until Europeans
came, there were neither horses, donkeys, sheep,
goats, cats, nor cattle (except the buffalo) in either
America. It was the Spanish pioneers who gave
all these animals to the Pueblos. Nor did the Indians have milk, cheese, wheat, or metals of any
sort. So when we see a story in which any of
these things are mentioned, we may know that it
was made within the last three hundred and fifty
years — or that an old story has been modified to
include them.

There is one of these comparatively modern

nursery-tales which is designed to show the honesty and wisdom of the Burro.

Once Big-ears was coming alone from the farm of his master to Isleta, carrying a load of curd cheeses done up in buckskin bags. As he came through the hills he met a Coyote, who said:

"Friend Big-ears, what do you carry on your back?"

"I carry many cheeses for my master, friend Too-wháy-deh," answered the Burro.

"Then give me one, friend, for I am hunger-dying."

"No," said the Burro, "I cannot give you one, for my master would blame me — since they are not mine but his, and a man of the pueblo waits for them."

Many times the Coyote asked him, with soft words; but Big-ears would not, and went his way. Then Too-wháy-deh followed him behind, without noise, and slyly bit the bag and stole a cheese. But Big-ears did not know it, for he could not see behind.

When he came to the pueblo, the man who awaited him unloaded the cheeses and counted them. "There lacks one," he said; "for thy master said he would send *so* many. Where is the other?"

"Truly, I know not," answered Big-ears, "but I think Too-wháy-deh stole it; for he asked me on the way to give him a cheese. But wait — I will pay him!"

So Big-ears went back to the hills and looked for the house of Too-wháy-deh. At last he found it, but the Coyote was nowhere. So he lay down

near the hole, and stretched his legs out as if dead,
and opened his mouth wide, and was very still.

Time passing so, the Old-Woman-Coyote came
out of the house to bring a jar of water. But
when she saw the Burro lying there, she dropped
her *tinaja*, and ran in crying:

"*Hloo-hli!*[1] come out and see! For a *buffalo*
has died out here, and we must take in some meat."

So Old-Man-Coyote came out, and was very
glad, and began to sharpen his knife.

But his wife said: "But before you cut him up,
get me the liver, for I am very hungry"—and the
liver is that which all the foxes like best.

Then the Old-Man-Coyote, thinking to please
her, went into the Burro's mouth to get the liver;
but Big-ears shut his teeth on Too-wháy-deh's
head, and jumped up and ran home. The Old-
Woman-Coyote followed running, crying : "*Ay,
Nana!* Let go!" But Big-ears would not listen to her, and brought the thief to his master.
When the master heard what had been, he killed
the Coyote, and thanked Big-ears, and gave him
much grass. And this is why, ever since, Big-
ears strikes with his hind feet if anything comes
behind him slyly; for he remembers how Too-
wháy-deh stole the cheese.

[1] Old Man.

XVI

THE FEATHERED BARBERS

THE Coyote, one summer day, having taken a bath in the river, lay down in the hot sand to dry himself. While he was sleeping there, a crowd of Quails came along; and seeing that he was asleep, they said:

"Huh! Here is that foolish Too-wháy-deh. Let us give him a trick!"

So they cut off all his hair, which makes one to be laughed at, and ran away.

When the Coyote woke up he was ashamed, and wished to punish those who had made him *pelado;* and he ran around to see if he could find the tracks of an enemy. There were only the tracks of the Quails, so he knew they had done it. Very angry, he followed the trail until it went into a large hole. He went all around to see if they had not come out; but there were no other tracks, so he went in. First the hole was big, but then it grew small, and he had to dig. When he had dug a long time, he caught a Quail, and he said:

"Ho, Ch'um-níd-deh! It is you that cut my hair and left me a laughed-at. But I am going to eat you this very now!"

"No, friend Too-wháy-deh, it was another who did it. You will find him farther in, with the scissors[1] still in his hand."

So the Coyote let that Quail go, and dug and dug till he caught another. But that one said the same thing; and Too-wháy-deh let him go, and dug after the next one. So it was, until he had let them all go, one by one; and when he came to the very end of the hole, there were no more.

With this, the Coyote was very angry, and ran out of the hole, promising to catch and eat them all. As he came out he met the Cotton-tail, and cried with a fierce face:

"Hear, you Pee-oo-ée-deh! If you don't catch me the Ch'úm-nin that cut my hair, I 'll eat *you!*"

"Oh, I can catch them, friend Coyote," said the Rabbit. "See, here is their trail!"

When they had followed the trail a long way, they saw the birds sitting and laughing under a bush.

"Now you wait here while I go and catch them," said Pee-oo-ée-deh. So the Coyote sat down to rest. As soon as the Rabbit was near them, the Quails flew a little way, and he kept running after them. But as soon as they were over a little hill, he turned aside and ran home, and the Coyote never knew if the Quails were caught or not.

[1] This indicates that the tale is comparatively modern.

THE ACCURSED LAKE

XVII

AWAY to the southeast of the Manzano Mountains, two days' journey from my pueblo of Isleta, are the shallow salt lakes. For scores of miles their dazzling sheen is visible — a strange patch of silver on the vast brown plains. They are near the noblest ruins in our North America — the wondrous piles of massive masonry of Abó, Cuaray, and the so-called "Gran Quivira"—the latter the home of the silliest delusion that ever lured treasure-hunters to their death. The whole region has a romantic history, and is important to the scientific student. From that locality

came, centuries ago, part of the people who then
founded Isleta, and whose descendants dwell here
to this day. Perhaps you would like to know *why*
those lakes are salt now—for my Indian neighbors
say that once they were fresh and full of fish, and
that the deer and buffalo came from all the country
round to drink there. The story is very important
ethnologically, for it tells much of the strange secret religion of the Pueblos, and more concerning
the method of initiating a young Indian into one
of the orders of medicine-men—both matters which
men of science have found extremely difficult to
be learned. Here is the story as it is believed by
the Tée-wahn, and as it was related to me by one
of them.

Long ago there was still a village east of Shoo-
paht-hóo-eh, the Eagle-Feather (Manzano) Mountains, and in it lived a famous hunter. One day,
going out on the plains to the east, he stalked a
herd of antelopes, and wounded one with his arrows. It fled eastward, while the herd went south;
and the hunter began to trail it by the drops of
blood. Presently he came to the largest lake, into
which the trail led. As he stood on the bank, wondering what to do, a fish thrust its head from the
water and said:

"Friend Hunter, you are on dangerous ground!"
and off it went swimming. Before the Hunter
could recover from his surprise, a Lake-Man came
up out of the water and said:

"How is it that you are here, where no human
ever came?"

10

The Hunter told his story, and the Lake-Man invited him to come in. When he had entered the lake, he came to a house with doors to the east, north, west, and south, and a trap-door in the roof, with a ladder; and by the latter door they entered. In their talk together the Lake-Man learned that the Hunter had a wife and little son at home.

"If that is so," said he, "why do you not come and live with me? I am here alone, and have plenty of other food, but I am no hunter. We could live very well here together." And opening doors on four sides of the room he showed the Hunter four other huge rooms, all piled from floor to ceiling with corn and wheat and dried squash and the like.

"That is a very good offer," said the astonished Hunter. "I will come again in four days; and if my Cacique will let me, I will bring my family and stay."

So the Hunter went home—killing an antelope on the way—and told his wife all. She thought very well of the offer; and he went to ask permission of the Cacique. The Cacique demurred, for this was the best hunter in all the pueblo,[1] but at last consented and gave him his blessing.

So on the fourth day the Hunter and his wife and little boy came to the lake with all their property. The Lake-Man met them cordially, and gave the house and all its contents into the charge of the woman.[2]

Some time passed very pleasantly, the Hunter going out daily and bringing back great quantities

---

[1] All hunters give the Cacique a tenth of their game, for his support.
[2] As is the custom among all Pueblo Indians.

THE HUNTER AND THE LAKE-MAN.

of game. . At last the Lake-Man, who was of an
evil heart, pretended to show the Hunter something in the east room; and pushing him in, locked
the great door and left him there to starve—for
the room was full of the bones of men whom he
had already entrapped in the same way.

The boy was now big enough to use his bow
and arrows so well that he brought home many
rabbits; and the witch-hearted Lake-Man began
to plot to get him, too, out of the way.

So one morning when the boy was about to
start for a hunt, he heard his mother groaning as
if about to die; and the Lake-Man said to him:

"My boy, your mother has a terrible pain, and
the only thing that will cure her is some ice from
T'hoor-p'ah-whée-ai [Lake of the Sun],[1] the water
from which the sun rises."

"Then," said the boy, straightway, "if that is so,
I will take the heart of a man [that is, be brave]
and go and get the ice for my little mother." And
away he started toward the unknown east.

Far out over the endless brown plains he trudged
bravely; until at last he came to the house of Shee-
chóo-hlee-oh, the Old-Woman-Mole, who was there
all alone—for her husband had gone to hunt.
They were dreadfully poor, and the house was almost falling down, and the poor, wrinkled Old-
Woman-Mole sat huddled in the corner by the
fireplace, trying to keep warm by a few dying
coals. But when the boy knocked, she rose and
welcomed him kindly and gave him all there was
in the house to eat—a wee bowl of soup with a

1 Located "somewhere to the east"; perhaps the ocean.

patched-up snowbird in it. The boy was very hungry, and picking up the snowbird bit a big piece out of it.

"Oh, my child!" cried the old woman, beginning to weep. "You have ruined me! For my husband trapped that bird these many years ago, but we could never get another; and that is all we have had to eat ever since. So we never bit it, but cooked it over and over and drank the broth. And now not even that is left." And she wept bitterly.

"Nay, Grandmother, do not worry," said the boy. "Have you any long hairs?"—for he saw many snowbirds lighting near by.

"No, my child," said the old woman sadly. "There is no other living animal here, and you are the first human that ever came here."

But the boy pulled out some of his own long hair and made snares, and soon caught many birds. Then the Old-Woman-Mole was full of joy; and having learned his errand, she said:

"My son, fear not, for I will be the one that shall help you. When you come into the house of the Trues, they will tempt you with a seat; but you must sit down only on what you have.[1] Then they will try you with smoking the *weer*, but I will help you."

Then she gave him her blessing, and the boy started away to the east. At last, after a weary, weary way, he came so near the Sun Lake, that the *Whit-lah-wíd-deh*[2] of the Trues saw him coming, and went in to report.

---

[1] That is, upon his blanket and moccasins, the unvarying etiquette of the Medicine House.

[2] One of an order of medicine-men, who among other duties, act as guards of the Medicine House.

"Let him be brought in," said the Trues; and the Whit-lah-wíd-deh took the boy in and in through eight rooms, until he stood in the presence of all the gods, in a vast room. There were all the gods of the East, whose color is white, and the blue gods of the North, the yellow gods of the West, the red gods of the South, and the rainbow-colored gods of the Up, the Down, and the Center, all in human shape. Beyond their seats were all the sacred animals — the buffalo, the bear, the eagle, the badger, the mountain lion, the rattlesnake, and all the others that are powerful in medicine.

Then the Trues bade the boy sit down, and offered him a white *manta* (robe) for a seat; but he declined respectfully, saying that he had been taught, when in the presence of his elders, to sit on nothing save what he brought, and he sat upon his blanket and moccasins. When he had told his story, the Trues tried him, and gave him the sacred *weer* to smoke—a hollow reed rammed with *pee-en-hleh*.[1] He smoked, and held the smoke bravely. But just then the Old-Woman-Mole, who had followed him underground all this way, dug a hole up to his very toes; and the smoke went down through his feet into the hole, and away back to the Old-Woman-Mole's house, where it poured out in a great cloud. And not the tiniest particle escaped into the room of the Trues. He finished the second *weer*[2] without being sick at all; and the

[1] The smoking of the pungent *weer* is a very severe ordeal; and it is a disgrace to let any of the smoke escape from the mouth or nose.

[2] Two being the usual number given a candidate for initiation into a medicine order.

Trues said, "Yes, he is our son. But we will try him once more." So they put him into the room of the East with the bear and the lion; and the savage animals came forward and breathed on him, but would not hurt him. Then they put him into the room of the North, with the eagle and the hawk; then into the room of the West, with the snakes; and lastly, into the room of the South, where were the Apaches and all the other human enemies of his people. And from each room he came forth unscratched.

"Surely," said the Trues, "this is our son! But once more we will try him."

They had a great pile of logs built up ("cob-house" fashion), and the space between filled with pine-knots. Then the Whit-lah-wíd-deh set the boy on the top of the pile and lighted it.

But in the morning, when the guard went out, there was the boy unharmed and saying:. "Tell the Trues I am cold, and would like more fire."

Then he was brought again before the Trues, who said: "Son, you have proved yourself a True Believer, and now you shall have what you seek."

So the sacred ice was given him, and he started homeward — stopping on the way only to thank the Old-Woman-Mole, to whose aid he owed his success.

When the wicked Lake-Man saw the boy coming, he was very angry, for he had never expected him to return from that dangerous mission. But he deceived the boy and the woman; and in a few days made a similar excuse to send the boy to the gods of the South after more ice for his mother.

The boy started off as bravely as before. When he had traveled a great way to the south, he came to a drying lake; and there, dying in the mud, was a little fish.

"*Ah-bóo* [poor thing], little fish," said the boy; and picking it up, he put it in his gourd canteen of water. After awhile he came to a good lake; and as he sat down to eat his lunch the fish in his gourd said:

"Friend Boy, let me swim while you eat, for I love the water."

So he put the fish in the lake; and when he was ready to go on, the fish came to him, and he put it back in his gourd. At three lakes he let the fish swim while he ate; and each time the fish came back to him. But beyond the third lake began a great forest which stretched clear across the world, and was so dense with thorns and brush that no man could pass it. But as the boy was wondering what he should do, the tiny fish changed itself into a great Fish-Animal with a very hard, strong skin,[1] and bidding the boy mount upon its back, it went plowing through the forest, breaking down big trees like stubble, and bringing him through to the other side without a scratch.

"Now, Friend Boy," said the Fish-Animal, "you saved my life, and I will be the one that shall help you. When you come to the house

---

[1] It is quite possible that this "Fish-Animal with a hard, strong skin," living far to the south, is the alligator. Of course, the Pueblos never saw that strange saurian; but they probably heard of it in the earliest days from nomad tribes, and as a great scientist has pointed out, we may always depend upon it that there is a nucleus of truth in all these folk-myths. Such a strange animal, once heard of, would be very sure to figure in some story.

of the Trues, they will try you as they did in
the East. And when you have proved yourself,
the Cacique will bring you his three daughters,
from whom to choose you a wife. The two
eldest are very beautiful, and the youngest is
not; but you ought to choose her, for beauty
does not always reach to the heart."

The boy thanked his fish-friend and went on,
until at last he came to the house of the Trues of
the South. There they tried him with the *weer*
and the fire, just as the Trues of the East had
done, but he proved himself a man, and they gave
him the ice. Then the Cacique brought his three
daughters, and said:

"Son, you are now old enough to have a wife,[1]
and I see that you are a true man who will dare
all for his mother. Choose, therefore, one of my
daughters."

The boy looked at the three girls; and truly the
eldest were very lovely. But he remembered the
words of his fish friend, and said:

"Let the youngest be my wife."

Then the Cacique was pleased, for he loved
this daughter more than both the others. And
the boy and the Cacique's daughter were married
and started homeward, carrying the ice and many
presents.

When they came to the great forest, there was
the Fish-Animal waiting for them, and taking both
on his back he carried them safely through. At
the first lake he bade them good-by and blessed
them, and they trudged on alone.

1 For it must be remembered that all these travels had taken many years.

THE CURSING OF THE LAKE.

At last they came in sight of the big lake, and over it were great clouds, with the forked lightning leaping forth. While they were yet far off, they could see the wicked Lake-Man sitting at the top of his ladder, watching to see if the boy would return, and even while they looked they saw the lightning of the Trues strike him and tear him to shreds.

When they came to the lake the boy found his mother weeping for him as dead. And taking his wife and his mother,—but none of the things of .the Lake-Man, for those were bewitched,—the boy came out upon the shore. There he stood and prayed to the Trues that the lake might be accurst forever; and they heard his prayer, for from that day its waters turned salt, and no living thing has drunk therefrom.

XVIII

SOME of the folk-stories told in Isleta were evidently invented in other pueblos, whence the Tée-wahn have learned them in their trading-trips. There is even a story from the far-off towns of Moqui, three hundred miles west of here and ninety miles from the railroad. The Moquis live in northeast Arizona, in strange adobe towns,[2] perched upon impregnable islands of rock, rising far above the bare, brown plain. They are seldom visited and little known by white men. All the other Pueblo towns and tribes have changed somewhat in the present era of American occupation; but the Moquis remain very much as they were when the first Spaniard found them — three hundred and fifty years ago. They retain many customs long extinct among their kindred, and have some of which no trace is to be found elsewhere. One of the minor differences, but one which would be almost the first to strike a stranger, is the absence of captive eagles in Moqui; and this is explained by the following folk-story:

[1] Pronounced Móh-kee.
[2] See "Some Strange Corners of Our Country." The Century Co., New York.

The Eagle is Kah-báy-deh (commander) of all that flies, and his feathers are strongest in medicine.

So long ago that no man can tell how long, there lived in Moqui an old man and an old woman, who had two children — a boy and a girl. The boy, whose name was Tái-oh, had a pet Eagle, of which he was very fond; and the Eagle loved its young master. Despite his youth, Tái-oh was a capital hunter; and every day he brought home not only rabbits enough for the family, but also to keep the Eagle well fed.

One day when he was about to start on a hunt, he asked his sister to look out for the Eagle during his absence. No sooner was he out of sight than the girl began to upbraid the bird bitterly, saying: "How I hate you, for my brother loves you so much. If it were not for you, he would give me many more rabbits, but now you eat them up."

The Eagle, feeling the injustice of this, was angry; so when she brought him a rabbit for breakfast the Eagle turned his head and looked at it sidewise, and would not touch it. At noon, when she brought him his dinner, he did the same thing; and at night, when Tái-oh returned, the Eagle told him all that had happened.

"Now," said the Eagle, "I am very tired of staying always here in Moqui, and I want to go home to visit my people a little. Come and go along with me, that you may see where the Eagle-people live."

"It is well," replied Tái-oh. "To-morrow morning we will go together."

In the morning they all went out into the fields, far down in the valley, to hoe their corn, leaving Tái-oh at home.

"Now," said the Eagle, "untie this thong from my leg, friend, and get astride my neck, and we will go."

The string was soon untied, and Tái-oh got astride the neck of the great bird, which rose up into the air as though it carried no weight at all. It circled over the town a long time, and the people cried out with wonder and fear at seeing an Eagle with a boy on his back. Then they sailed out over the fields, where Tái-oh's parents and his sister were at work; and all the three began to cry, and went home in great sorrow.

The Eagle kept soaring up and up until they came to the very sky. There in the blue was a little door, through which the Eagle flew. Alighting on the floor of the sky, he let Tái-oh down from his back, and said:

"Now, you wait here, friend, while I go and see my people," and off he flew.

Tái-oh waited three days, and still the Eagle did not return; so he became uneasy and started out to see what he could find. After wandering a long way, he met an old Spider-woman.

"Where are you going, my son?" she asked.

"I am trying to find my friend, the Eagle."

"Very well, then, I will help you. Come into my house."

"But how can I come into so small a door?" objected Tái-oh.

"Just put your foot in, and it will open big enough for you to enter."

So Tái-oh put his foot in, and, sure enough, the door opened wide, and he went into the Spider's house and sat down.

"Now," said she, "you will have some trouble in getting to the house of your friend, the Eagle, for to get there you will have to climb a dreadful ladder. It is well that you came to me for help, for that ladder is set with sharp arrow-heads and knives of flint, so that if you tried to go up it, it would cut your legs off. But I will give you this sack of sacred herbs to help you. When you come to the ladder, you must chew some of the herbs and spit the juice on the ladder, which will at once become smooth for you."[1]

Tái-oh thanked the Spider-woman and started off with the sack. After awhile he came to the foot of a great ladder, which went away up out of sight. Its sides and rungs were bristling with keen arrow-heads, so that no living thing could climb it; but when Tái-oh chewed some of the magic herb and spat upon the ladder, all the sharp points fell off, and it was so smooth that he climbed it without a single scratch.

After a long, long climb, he came to the top of the ladder, and stepped upon the roof of the Eagles' house. But when he came to the door he found it so bristling with arrow-points that whoever might try to enter would be cut to pieces. Again he chewed some of the herb, and spat upon the door;

[1] This recalls a superstition of the Peruvian mountain Indians, ancient and modern. The latter I have often seen throwing upon a stone at the crest of a mountain pass the quid of coca-leaves they had been chewing. They believe such use of this sacred herb propitiates the spirits and keeps off the terrible *soroche*, or mountain-sickness; and that it also makes veins of metal easier to be worked — softening the stone, even as it did for Tái-oh.

and at once all the points fell off, and he entered safely, and inside he found his Eagle-friend, and all the Eagle-people. His friend had fallen in love with an Eagle-girl and married her, and that was the reason he had not returned sooner.

Tái-oh stayed there some time, being very nicely entertained, and enjoyed himself greatly in the strange sky-country. At last one of the wise old Eagle-men came to him and said:

"Now, my son, it is well that you go home, for your parents are very sad, thinking you are dead. After this, whenever you seen an Eagle caught and kept captive, you must let it go; for now you have been in our country, and know that when we come home we take off our feather-coats and are people like your own."

So Tái-oh went to his Eagle-friend and said he thought he must go home.

"Very well," said the Eagle; "get on my neck and shut your eyes, and we will go."

So he got on, and they went down out of the sky, and down and down until at last they came to Moqui. There the Eagle let Tái-oh down among the wondering people, and, bidding him an affectionate good-by, flew off to his young wife in the sky.

Tái-oh went to his home loaded down with dried meat and tanned buckskin, which the Eagle had given him; and there was great rejoicing, for all had given him up as dead. And this is why, to this very day, the Moquis will not keep an Eagle captive, though nearly all the other Pueblo towns have all the Eagle-prisoners they can get.

XIX

NEARLY every nation has its folk-lore concerning Jack Frost and his anti-type. The cold
North Wind is always the enemy of man, and the
warm South Wind always his friend. The Quères
pueblos of Acoma and Laguna have an allegorical
folk-story, in which the good spirit of heat defeats
his icy-hearted rival.

Once, long ago, the *ta-pó-pe* (governor) of
Acoma had a beautiful daughter, for whom many
of the young men had asked in vain, for she would
have none of them. One day there came climbing
up the stone ladder to the cliff-built pueblo a tall
and handsome stranger. His dress glistened with
white crystals, and his face, though handsome, was
very stern. The fair *kot-chin-á-ka* (chief's daughter), bending at a pool in the great rock to fill her
water-jar, saw and admired him as he came strid-
ing proudly to the village; and he did not fail to
notice the dusky beauty. Soon he asked for her in
due form; and in a little while they were to be
married.

But, with the coming of Shó-kee-ah — for that
was the name of the handsome stranger — a sad

change befell Acoma. The water froze in the
springs and the corn withered in the fields. Every
morning Shó-kee-ah left the town and went away
to his home in the far North; and every evening
he returned, and the air grew chill around. The
people could raise no crops, for the bitter· cold
killed all that they planted, and nothing would grow
but the thorny cactus. To keep from starving,
they had to eat the cactus-leaves, roasting them
first to remove the sharp thorns. One day, when
the *kot-chin-á-ka* was roasting cactus-leaves, there
came another handsome stranger with a sunny
smile and stood beside her.

"What dost thou there?" he asked; and she
told him.

"But do not so," said the young man, giving her
an ear of green corn. "Eat this, and I will bring
thee more."

So saying, he was gone; but very soon he returned with such a load of green corn as the
strongest man could not lift, and carried it to
her house.

"Roast this," he said, "and when the people
come to thee, give them each two ears, for hereafter
there shall always be much corn."

She roasted the corn and gave it to the people,
who took it eagerly, for they were starving. But
soon Shó-kee-ah returned, and the warm, bright
day grew suddenly cold and cloudy. As he
put his foot on the ladder to come down into the
house (all Pueblo rooms used to be entered only
from the roof, and thousands are so yet) great
flakes of snow fell around him; but Mí-o-chin,

the newcomer, made it very warm, and the snow melted.

"Now," said Shó-kee-ah, "we will see which is more powerful; and he that is shall have the *kot-chin-á-ka*." Mí-o-chin accepted the challenge, and it was agreed that the contest should begin on the morrow and last three days. Mí-o-chin went to consult an old Spider-woman as to the best way to conquer his powerful rival, and she gave him the necessary advice.

Next day the people all gathered to see the trial of strength between the two wizards. Shó-kee-ah "made medicine," and caused a driving sleet and a bitter wind that froze all waters. But Mí-o-chin built a fire and heated small stones in it, and with them caused a warm South Wind, which melted the ice. On the second day, Shó-kee-ah used more powerful incantations, and made a deep snow to cover the world; but again Mí-o-chin brought his South Wind and chased away the snow. On the third day Shó-kee-ah used his strongest spell, and it rained great icicles, until everything was buried under them. But when Mí-o-chin built his fire and heated the stones, again the warm South Wind drove away the ice and dried the earth. So it remained to Mí-o-chin; and the defeated Shó-kee-ah went away to his frozen home in the North, leaving Mí-o-chin to live happy ever after with the *kot-chin-á-ka*, whom he married amid the rejoicing of all the people of Acoma.

XX

THE TOWN OF THE SNAKE-GIRLS

IN the times that were farthest back, the fore-fathers of those who now dwell in Isleta were scattered about in many small villages. You have already heard the myths of how the inhabitants of several villages finally abandoned their homes and came to live in the one big town of the Tée-wahn. Three miles north of Isleta, amid the sandy plain of Los Padillas, stands the strange round mesa of Shee-em-tóo-ai. It is a circular "island" of hard, black lava, cut off from the long lava cliffs which wall the valley of the Rio Grande on the west. Its level top, of over fifty acres, is some two hundred feet above the plain; the last fifty feet being a stern and almost unbroken cliff. Upon its top are still visible the crumbling ruins of the pueblo of Poo-reh-tú-ai — a town deserted, as we are histori-cally sure, over three hundred and fifty years ago. The mound outlines of the round *estufa*, the houses and the streets, are still easy to be traced, and bits of pottery, broken arrow-heads, and other relics, still abound there. In history we know no more of the pueblo than that it was once there, but had been abandoned already when Coronado passed in

1540; but my aboriginal friends and fellow-citizens of Shee-eh-whíb-bahk have an interesting legend of the pueblo of Poo-reh-tú-ai and the cause which led to its abandonment.

When the mesa town was inhabited, so was Isleta; and, being but three miles apart, the inter-communication was constant. At one time, four hundred years ago or more, there lived in Isleta a very handsome youth whose name was K'oo-ah-máh-koo-hóo-oo-aí-deh—which means Young-Man-Who-Embraces-a-Corncob.

In spite of this serious burden of a title, the young man was greatly admired, and had many friends. Probably they called him something else "for short," or people would n't have had time to associate with him. There were two sisters, very pretty girls, living in Poo-reh-tú-ai, and they fell very seriously in love, both with this same youth. But he had never really found out how handsome he was, and so thought little about girls anyhow, caring more to run fastest in the races and to kill the most game in the hunts. The sisters, finding that he would not notice their shy smiles, began to make it in their way to pass his house whenever they came to Isleta, and to say *hin-a-kú-pui-yoo* (good morning) as they met him on the road. But he paid no attention to them whatever, except to be polite; and even when they sent him the modest little gift which means "there is a young lady who loves you!" he was as provokingly in-different as ever.

After long coquetting in vain, the girls began to hate him as hard as before they had loved him.

They decided, no doubt, that he was *oó-teh*, the Tée-wahn word for "a mean old thing"; and finally one proposed that they put him out of the way, for both sisters, young and pretty as they were, were witches.

"We will teach him," said one.

"Yes," said the other, "he ought to be punished; but how shall we do it?"

"Oh, we will invite him to play a game of *mahkhúr*, and then we'll fix him. I'll go now and make the hoop."

The witch-sisters made a very gay hoop, and then sent word to the youth to meet them at the sacred sand-hill, just west of Isleta, as they had important business with him. Wondering what it could be, he met them at the appointed time and place.

"Now, Brother Young-Man-Who-Embraces-a-Corncob," said the eldest sister, "we want to amuse ourselves a little, so let us have a game of *mahkhúr*. We have a very nice hoop to play it. You go half-way down the hill and see if you can catch it when we roll it to you. If you can, you may have the hoop; but if you fail, you come and roll it to us and we'll see if we can catch it."

So he wént down the hill and waited, and the girls sent the bright wheel rolling toward him. He was very nimble, and caught it "on the fly"; but that very instant he was no longer the tall, handsome Young-Man-Who-Embraces-a-Corncob, but a poor little Coyote, with great tears rolling down his cheeks. The witch-sisters came laughing and taunting him, and said:

"You see it would have been better to marry us! But now you will always be a Coyote and an outcast from home. You may roam to the north and to the south and to the west, but never to the east" (and therefore not back to Isleta).

The Coyote started off, still weeping; and the two wicked sisters went home rejoicing at their success. The Coyote roamed away to the west, and at last turned south. After a time he came across a party of Isleteños[1] returning from a trading-trip to the Apache country. He sneaked about their camp, snapping up odd scraps—for he was nearly starved. In the morning the Indians spied this Coyote sitting and watching them at a little distance, and they set their dogs on him. But the Coyote did not run; and when the dogs came to him they merely sniffed and came away without hurting him—though every one knows that the dog and the Coyote have been enemies almost ever since the world began. The Indians were greatly astonished; and one of them, who was a medicine-man, began to suspect that there was something wrong. So, without saying anything to the others, he walked over to the Coyote and said: "Coyote, are you Coyote-true, or somebody bewitched?" But the Coyote made no reply. Again the medicine-man asked: "Coyote, are you a man?" At this the Coyote nodded his head affirmatively, while tears rolled from his eyes.

"Very well, then," said the medicine-man, "come with me." So the Coyote rose and followed him to the camp; and the medicine-man fed and cared

---

[1] Pronounced Eez-lay-táyn-yos.

for him as the party journeyed toward Isleta. The last night they camped at the big barranca, just below the village; and here the medicine-man told his companions the story of the bewitchment,—for the Coyote had already told him,—and they were all greatly astonished, and very sad to learn that this poor Coyote was their handsome friend, K'co-ah-máh-koo-hóo-oo-aí-deh.

"Now," said the medicine-man, "we will make a nice hoop and try a game." He made it, and said to the Coyote: "Friend, go and stand over there; and when I roll this hoop toward you, you must jump and put your head through it before it stops rolling or falls over upon its side."

The Coyote stood off, and the medicine-man sent the hoop rolling toward him very hard. Just as it came near enough the Coyote made a wonderful jump and put his head squarely through the middle of it—and there, instead of the gaunt Coyote, stood the Young-Man-Who-Embraces-a-Corn-cob, handsome and well and strong as ever. They all crowded around to congratulate him and to listen to what had befallen him.

"Now," said the medicine-man, "when we get home, the two witch-sisters will come to congratulate you, and will pretend not to know anything of the trouble that befell you, and when you see them you must invite *them* to a game of *mah-khúr*."

It all came about as he said. When the party got back to Isleta all the people welcomed the young man whose mysterious disappearance had made all sad. The news of his return spread rapidly, and soon reached the village of Poo-reh-tú-ai.

In a day or two the witch-sisters came to Isleta, bringing on their heads baskets of the choicest foods and other gifts, which they presented to him in the most cordial manner. To see how they welcomed him, one would never fancy that they had been the wicked causes of his suffering. He played his part equally well, and gave no sign that he saw through their duplicity. At last, when they were about to start home, he said: " Sisters, let us come to the sand-hill to-morrow to play a little game."

An invitation—or rather a challenge—of that sort must be accepted under all Indian etiquette; and the witch-sisters agreed. So at the appointed hour they met him at the sacred hill. He had made a very beautiful hoop, and when they saw it they were charmed, and took their positions at the foot of the declivity. " One, two, three !" he counted; and at the word " three !" sent the hoop rolling down to them. They both grabbed it at the same instant, and lo ! instead of the pretty, but evil-minded sisters of Poo-reh-tú-ai, there lay two huge rattlesnakes, with big tears falling from their eyes. Young-Man-Who-Embraces-a-Corncob laid upon their ugly, flat heads a pinch of the sacred meal, and they ran out their tongues and licked it.

"Now," he said, "this is what happens to the treacherous. Here in these cliffs shall be your home forever. You must never go to the river, so you will suffer with thirst and drag yourselves in the dust all the days of your life."

The Young-Man-Who-Embraces-a-Corncob went back to Isleta, where he lived to a ripe old

age. As for the snakes, they went to live in the
cliffs of their own mesa. The people of Poo-reh-
tú-ai soon learned of the fate of the witch-sisters,
and knew that those two great snakes, with tears
in their eyes, were they. That was the beginning of
the downfall of Poo-reh-tú-ai; for the people grew
fearful of one another, lest there might be many
more witches, unbeknown, among them. The dis-
trust and discontent grew rapidly — for to this day
nothing on earth will disrupt any Indian community so quickly or so surely as the belief that some
of the people are witches. In a very short time
the people decided to abandon Poo-reh-tú-ai altogether. Most of them migrated to the Northwest,
and I have not as yet found even a legend to tell
what became of them. The rest settled in Isleta,
where their descendants dwell to this day. There
are old men here now who claim that their great-
grandfathers used to see the two huge rattle-
snakes basking on the cliffs of the mesa of Shee-
em-tóo-ai, and that the snakes always wept when
people came near them.

XXI

THE DROWNING OF PECOS

TWENTY-FIVE miles southeast of Santa Fé, New Mexico, lie the deserted ruins of the ancient Pueblo town of Pecos. The village was finally abandoned by the Indians in 1840; and their neat houses of adobe bricks and stone, and their quaint adobe church, have sadly fallen to decay. The history of the abandonment of Pecos is by no means startling; but the Indian tradition — for they have already added this to their countless myths — is decidedly so. The story is related by two aged Pecos Indians who still live in the pueblo of Jemez.

"Now, this is a true story," said my informant, an Isleteño, who had often heard it from them.

Once Pecos was a large village, and had many people.[1] But it came that nearly all of them had the evil road, and in the whole town were but five True Believers (in the Indian religion). These were an old woman, her two sons, and two other young men. Agostin, her elder son, was a famous

---

[1] It was, indeed, the largest pueblo in New Mexico, having at one time a population of about 2000.

hunter, and very often went to the mountains with a friend of his who had an evil spirit — though Agostin was not aware of that.

One day the friend invited Agostin to go hunting, and next day they went to the mountains. Just at the foot they found a herd of deer, one of which Agostin wounded. The deer fled up the mountain, and the two friends followed by the drops of blood. Half-way to the top they came to a second herd, which ran off to the right of the trail they were following, and the evil-spirited friend went in pursuit of them, while Agostin kept on after the one he had wounded.

He came at last to the very top of the mountain, and there of a sudden the trail ceased. Agostin hunted all about, but in vain, and at last started down the other side of the mountain.

As he came to a deep cañon he heard singing, and, peering cautiously through the bushes, he saw a lot of witch-men sitting around a fallen pine and singing, while their chief was trying to raise the tree.

Agostin recognized them all, for they were of Pecos, and he was much grieved when he saw his friend among them. Then he knew that the deer had all been witches, and that they had led him off on a false trail.

Greatly alarmed, he crept back to a safe distance, and then hurried home and told his aged mother all that had happened, asking her if he should report it to the Cacique.

"No," said she, with a sigh, "it is of no use; for he, too, has the evil road. There are but few

True Believers left, and the bad ones are trying
to use us up."

Among the five good people was one of the
Cum-pah-whit-lah-wen (guards of the medicine-
men); and to him Agostin told his story. But he
also said: "It is of no use. We are too few to do
anything."

At last the bad people falsely accused the old
woman, saying that her power was more than that
of all the medicine-men put together (which is a
very serious charge, even to-day, among the Indians); and challenged her to come before all the
people in the medicine-house and perform miracles
with them, well knowing that she could not. The
challenge was for life or death; whichever side
won was to kill the others without being resisted.

The poor old woman told her sons, with tears,
saying: "Already we are killed. We know nothing of these things, and we may make ready to die."

"Nay, Nana," said Agostin.[1] "Despair not yet,
but prepare lunch for Pedro[1] and me, that we go to
other villages for advice. Perhaps there the medicine-men will tell us something."

So the mother, still weeping, made some tortillas, and, strapping these to their belts, the young
men set out.

Pedro, the younger, went east, and Agostin took
the road to the north. Whatever person they met,
or to whatever village they came, they were to seek
advice.

When Agostin came to the foot of the mountains,
he was very thirsty, but there was no water. As he

[1] Pronounced Ah-gohs-téen and Páy-droh.

entered a gorge he saw H'yo-kwáh-kwah-báy-deh, a little bird which builds its nest with pebbles and clay in the crannies of the cliffs, and is of exactly the same color as the sandstones. He thought, "Ah, little bird, if you could speak I would ask you where there is water, for I am fainting with thirst, and dare not eat, for that would make it worse!"

But the little bird, knowing his thought, said:

"Friend Agostin, I see that you are one of the True Believers, and I will show you where there is water; or wait, I will go and bring you some, for it is very far." And off he flew.

Agostin waited, and presently the little bird came back, bringing an acorn-cup·full of water. Then Agostin's heart sank, and he thought: "Alas! what good will that drop do me?"

But the little bird replied: "Do not think that way, friend. Here is enough, and even more; for when you drink all you wish, there will still be some left."

And so it was. Agostin drank and drank, then ate some tortillas and drank again; and when he was satisfied, the acorn-cup was still nearly full.

Then the little bird said: "Now come, and I will lead you. But when we come to the top of the mountain, and I say, 'We are at the top,' you must say, 'No, we are down in the mountain—at the bottom of it.' Do not forget."

Agostin promised, and the little bird flew in front of him. At last they were at the top, and the little bird said:

"Here we are, friend, at the top."

"No," answered Agostin, "we are down in the mountain—at the bottom of it."

Three times the little bird repeated his words, and three times Agostin made the same answer.

At the third reply they found themselves in a room in the mountain. There was a door in front of them, and beside it stood a Cum-pah-whit-lah-wíd-deh (guard), who said to Agostin—for the little bird had disappeared:

"Son, how came you here, where none ever think of coming? Do you think you are a man?"

Agostin told the whole story of the witches' challenge, and of how he had gone out to seek advice, and of how the little bird had brought him here, and the guard said:

"You are coming with the thought of a man; so now come in," and he opened the door.

But when Agostin entered the inner room, which was so large that no end could be seen, he found himself in the presence of the Trues in human shape.

There sat the divinities of the East, who are white; and of the North, who are blue; and beyond them were the sacred animals—the mountain lion, the eagle, bear, buffalo, badger, hawk, rabbit, rattlesnake, and all the others that are of the Trues. Agostin was very much afraid, but the guard said to him:

"Do not fear, son, but take the heart of a man, and pray to all sides." So he faced to the six sides, praying. When he had finished, one of the Trues spoke to him, and said:

"What can it be that brought you here? Take the heart of a man and tell us."

Then Agostin told his whole story; after which the Trues said to him:

"Do not be worried, son. We will help you out of that."

The principal True of the East said:

"Son, I will give you the clothes you must wear when you are in the medicine-house for the contest of power"; and he gave Agostin four dark-blue breech-clouts and some moccasins for himself and the three other good young men, and a black *manta* (robe) and pair of moccasins for his mother.

"Now," said the True, "the evil-spirited ones will have this medicine-making contest in the *es-tufa*,[1] and when you enter, you five, you must all be dressed in these clothes. The people will all be there, old and young, and there will hardly be room for you to stand; and they will all sneer at you and spit upon you. But do not be sorry. And take this cane to hold between you. Let your mother take it with one hand at the bottom, then the Whit-lah-wíd-deh's hand, then her other hand, and then his other hand; and last your brother's hand, your hand, then his other hand, and your other hand at the top of all. And when you say, 'We are at the top of the mountain,' he must answer, 'No, we are down in the mountain—at the bottom of it.' This you must keep saying. Now go, son, with the heart of a man."

Then the Whit-lah-wíd-deh led Agostin out, and the little bird showed him the way down the mountain.

When he reached home it was the afternoon of

---

[1] Where it is sacrilegious to make medicine.

the appointed day, and in the evening the medicine-making contest for life or death was to come.

In a little while the younger brother arrived,
with his new clothes and moccasins torn to shreds;
for he had traveled far in a rough country, without
meeting a soul from whom to ask advice.

Agostin called together the four other True Believers, and told them all that had happened and
what they must do, giving them the sacred clothing.

In the evening they went to the *estufa*, which
was crowded with the witch-people, so that they
had barely room to stand.

Then the evil-spirited ones began to make medicine, and turned themselves into bears, coyotes,
crows, owls, and other animals. When they were
done, they said to the old woman :

"Now it is your turn. We will see what you
can do."

"I know nothing about these things," she said, "but
I will do what I can, and the Trues will help me."

Then she and the four young men took hold of
the sacred cane as the Trues had showed Agostin.

"We are on the top of the mountain," said he.

"No," answered his brother, "we are down in
the mountain—at the bottom of it."

This they said three times. At the third saying
the people heard on all sides the *guajes* of the
Trues.[1] At the same moment the ladder[2] was
jerked violently up out of the room, so that no
one could get out.

[1] The thunder is said by the Tée-wahn to be the sacred dance-rattle of
their gods.
[2] The only entrance to any *estufa* is by a ladder let down through a door
in the roof.

Then the two brothers repeated their words again, and at the third saying the thunder began to roar outside, and all could hear plainly the singing and the *guajes* of the Trues. It began to rain violently, and the water poured down through the roof-door, and the lightning stuck its tongue in. The brothers kept repeating their words, and soon the water was knee-deep. But where the five True Believers stood, holding the cane, the floor was dusty. Soon the flood came to the waists of the witch-people, and then to their necks, and the children were drowning. Then they cried out to the old woman:

"Truly, mother, your power is greater than ours. We submit."

But she paid no attention to them, and her sons continued their words, and the water kept pouring in until it touched the very ceiling. But all around the five it stood back like a wall, and they were on dry ground.

At last all the evil-spirited ones were drowned. Then the rain ceased and the water departed as fast as it had come. The ladder came down through the roof-door again, and the five True Believers climbed out and went to their homes.

But it was very desolate, for they were the only survivors. Their nearest relatives and dearest friends had perished with the other witch-people. At last they could no longer bear to live in the lonely valley, and they decided to live elsewhere. On the way the old mother and one of the men died. Agostin went to the pueblo of Cochití, and Pedro and the Whit-lah-wíd-deh settled in the pueblo of Jemez, where they are still living (or were in the spring of 1891).

Such is the Indian version of the abandonment of the great pueblo which Coronado—that wonderful Spanish explorer—found in 1540. As a matter of fact, the Hyó-qua-hoon, or people of Pecos, had dwindled away by war, epidemics, and the like, until only five were left; and in 1840 these lonely survivors moved to other pueblos, and abandoned their ruined town forever. But the story is very valuable, not only for the glimpse it affords of some of their most secret beliefs, but also as showing how folk-stories of the most aboriginal stamp are still coined.

Witchcraft is still a serious trouble in all the pueblos, despite the efforts of the medicine-men, whose special duty it is to keep down the witches. One little pueblo called Sandia is dying out—as many others have done before it—because the medicine-men are quietly killing those whom they suspect of being witches. In 1888 a very estimable Indian woman of that town was slain by them in the customary way,—shot through from side to side with an arrow,—and this form of execution is still practised.

In Isleta they fear the Americans too much to indulge in witch-killing, for Albuquerque is only a few miles away. But it is only a little while ago that a young Isletan who was accused spent three months in the neck-stocks in our aboriginal prison, and much of the time had to "ride the horse," sitting with his legs crossed upon the adobe floor and the heavy weight of the stocks pressing him down,

13

a torture worthy of the Inquisition. The case was kept out of the American courts only by the payment of a large sum to his parents by his accusers.

One whose eyes or lids look red is always regarded with suspicion here, for witch-people are supposed not to sleep at night, but to change themselves into animals and roam over the world. Eccentric actions also lay one open to accusation; and when I first came here I was dangerously near being classed with the witches because, to amuse my dusky little neighbors, I imitated various animal cries to their great edification, but to the very serious doubt of their elders. The fact that they doubt whether Americans know enough to be first-class witches was largely instrumental in saving me from serious danger.

The Ants that Pushed on the Sky

XXII

A VERY ancient and characteristic story about the origin of Isleta is based on the historic fact that part of its founders came from east of the Manzano Mountains, from one of the prehistoric pueblos whose ruins are now barely visible in those broad plains.

Once upon a time there lived in one of those villages (so runs the story) a young Indian named Kahp-too-óo-yoo, the Corn-stalk Young Man. He was not only a famous hunter and a brave warrior against the raiding Comanches, but a great wizard; and to him the Trues had given the power of the clouds. When Kahp-too-óo-yoo willed it, the glad rains fell, and made the dry fields laugh in green;

and without him no one could bring water from
the sky. His father was Old-Black-Cane, his
mother was Corn-Woman, and his two sisters were
Yellow-Corn-Maiden, and Blue-Corn-Maiden.

Kahp-too-óo-yoo had a friend, a young man of
about the same age. But, as is often true, the
friend was of a false heart, and was really a witch,
though Kahp-too-óo-yoo never dreamed of such a
thing.

The two young men used to go together to the
mountains to get wood, and always carried their
bows and arrows, to kill deer and antelopes, or
whatever game they might find.

One day the false friend came to Kahp-too-óo-
yoo, and said:

"Friend, let us go to-morrow for wood, and to
hunt."

They agreed that so they would do. Next day
they started before sunrise, and came presently to
the spot where they gathered wood. Just there
they started a herd of deer. Kahp-too-óo-yoo
followed part of the herd, which fled to the northwest, and the friend pursued those that went southwest. After a long, hard chase, Kahp-too-óo-yoo
killed a deer with his swift arrows, and brought it
on his strong back to the place where they had
separated. Presently came the friend, very hot
and tired, and with empty hands; and seeing the
deer, he was pinched with jealousy.

"Come, friend," said Kahp-too-óo-yoo. "It is
well for brothers to share with brothers. Take of
this deer and cook and eat; and carry a part to
your house, as if you had killed it yourself."

"Thank you," answered the other coldly, as one who will not; but he did not accept.

When they had gathered each a load of wood, and lashed it with rawhide thongs in bundles upon their shoulders, they trudged home—Kahp-too-óo-yoo carrying the deer on top of his wood. His sisters received him with joy, praising him as a hunter; and the friend went away to his house, with a heavy face.

Several different days when they went to the mountain together, the very same thing came to pass. Kahp-too-óo-yoo killed each time a deer; and each time the friend came home with nothing, refusing all offers to share as brothers. And he grew more jealous and more sullen every day.

At last he came again to invite Kahp-too-óo-yoo to go; but this time it was with an evil purpose that he asked. Then again the same things happened. Again the unsuccessful friend refused to take a share of Kahp-too-óo-yoo's deer; and when he had sat long without a word, he said:

"Friend Kahp-too-óo-yoo, now I will prove you if you are truly my friend, for I do not think it."

"Surely," said Kahp-too-óo-yoo, "if there is any way to prove myself, I will do it gladly, for truly I am your friend."

"Then come, and we will play a game together, and with that I will prove you."

"It is well! But what game shall we play, for here we have nothing?"

Near them stood a broken pine-tree, with one great arm from its twisted body. And looking at it, the false friend said:

"I see nothing but to play the *gallo* race; and because we have no horses[1] we will ride this arm of the pine-tree—first I will ride, and then you."

So he climbed the pine-tree, and sat astride the limb as upon a horse, and rode, reaching over to the ground as if to pick up the chicken.[2]

"Now you," he said, coming down; and Kahp-too-óo-yoo climbed the tree and rode on the swinging branch. But the false friend bewitched the pine, and suddenly it grew in a moment to the very sky, carrying Kahp-too-óo-yoo.

"We do this to one another," taunted the false friend, as the tree shot up; and taking the wood, and the deer which Kahp-too-óo-yoo had killed, he went to the village. There the sisters met him, and asked:

"Where is our brother?"

"Truly I know not, for he went northwest and I southwest; and though I waited long at the meeting-place, he did not come. Probably he will soon return. But take of this deer which I killed, for sisters should share the labors of brothers."

But the girls would take no meat, and went home sorrowful.

Time went on, and still there was no Kahp-too-óo-yoo. His sisters and his old parents wept always, and all the village was sad. And soon the crops grew yellow in the fields, and the springs failed, and the animals walked like weary shadows; for Kahp-too-óo-yoo, he who had the power of the

---

[1] This mention of the horse is, of course, modern. I think it is an interpolation. The rest of the story bears traces of great antiquity.

[2] In imitation of one of the most popular and exciting sports of the Southwestern Indians and Mexicans.

clouds, was gone, and there was no rain. And then perished all that is green; the animals fell in the brown fields; and the gaunt people who sat to warm themselves in the sun began to die there where they sat. At last the poor old man said to his daughters:

"Little daughters, prepare food, for again we will go to look for your brother."

The girls made cakes of the blue corn-meal for the journey; and on the fourth day they started. Old-Black-Cane hobbled to the south, his wife to the east, the elder girl to the north, and the younger to the west.

For a great distance they traveled; and at last Blue-Corn-Maiden, who was in the north, heard a far, faint song. It was so little that she thought it must be imaginary; but she stopped to listen, and softly, softly it came again:

Tó-ai-fóo-ni-hlóo-hlim,
Eng-k'hai k'háhm ;
Eé-eh-bóori-kóon-hlee-oh,
Ing-k'hai k'háhm.
Ah-ee-ái, ah-hee-ái,
Aim !

(Old-Black-Cane
My father is called;
Corn-Woman
My mother is called.
Ah-ee-ái, ah-hee-ái,
Aim !)

When she heard this, Blue-Corn-Maiden ran until she came to her sister, and cried:

" Sister! Sister! I think I hear our brother somewhere in captivity.   Listen!"

Trembling, they listened; and again the song
came floating to them, so soft, so sad that they
wept—as to this day their people weep when a
white-haired old man, filled with the memories of
Kahp-too-óo-yoo, sings that plaintive melody.

"Surely it is our brother!" they cried; and off
they went running to find their parents.   And
when all listened together, again they heard the
song.

"Oh, my son!" cried the poor old woman, "in
what captivity do you find yourself? True it is
that your father is Old-Black-Cane, and I, your
mother, am called Corn-Woman.   But why do you
sing thus?"

Then all four of them began to follow the song,
and at last they came to the foot of the sky-reach-
ing pine; but they could see nothing of Kahp-too-
óo-yoo, nor could their cries reach him.   There, on
the ground, were his bow and arrows, with strings
and feathers eaten away by time; and there was
his pack of wood, tied with the rawhide thong,
ready to be taken home.   But after they had
searched everywhere, they could not find Kahp-
too-óo-yoo; and finally they went home heavy at
heart.

At last it happened that P'ah-whá-yoo-óo-deh,
the Little Black Ant, took a journey and went up
the bewitched pine, even to its top in the sky.
When he found Kahp-too-óo-yoo there a prisoner,
the Little Black Ant was astonished, and said:

"Great *Kah-báy-deh* [Man of Power], how comes

SOUTH, EAST, NORTH, AND WEST IN SEARCH OF KAHP-TOO-ÓO-YOO.

it that you are up here in such a condition, while
your people at home are suffering and dying for
rain, and few are left to meet you if you return?
Are you here of your free will?"

"No," groaned Kahp-too-óo-yoo; "I am here
because of the jealousy of him who was as my
brother, with whom I shared my food and labor,
whose home was my home, and my home his.   He
is the cause, for he was jealous and bewitched me
hither.   And now I am dying of famine."

"If that is so," said the Little Black Ant, "I will
be the one to help you"; and he ran down to the
world as fast as he could.   When he got there he
sent out the crier to summon all his nation, and
also that of the *In-toon*, the Big Red Ants.   Soon
all the armies of the Little Black Ants and the Big
Red Ants met at the foot of the pine, and held a
council.   They smoked the *weer* and deliberated
what should be done.

"You Big Red Ants are stronger than we who
are small," said the War-Captain of the Little
Black Ants, "and for that you ought to take the
top of the tree to work."

"*Een-dah!*" (No) said the War-Captain of the
Big Red Ants.   "If you think we are the stronger,
give us the bottom, where we can work more, and
you go to the top."

So it was agreed, and the captains made their
armies ready.   But first the Little Black Ants got
the cup of an acorn, and mixed in it corn-meal and
water and honey, and carried it up the tree.   They
were so many that they covered its trunk all the
way to the sky.

When Kahp-too-óo-yoo saw, his heart was heavy, and he thought: "But what good will that very little do me, for I am dying of hunger and thirst?" "Nay, friend," answered the Captain of the Little Black Ants, who knew his thought. "A person should not think so. This little is enough, and there will be some left."

And it was so; for when Kahp-too-óo-yoo had eaten all he could, the acorn-cup was still nearly full. Then the ants carried the cup to the ground and came back to him.

"Now, friend," said the Captain, "we will do our best. But now you must shut your eyes till I say '*Ahw!*'"

Kahp-too-óo-yoo shut his eyes, and the Captain sent signals down to those at the foot of the tree. And the Little Black Ants above put their feet against the sky and pushed with all their might on the top of the pine; and the Big Red Ants below caught the trunk and pulled as hard as they could; and the very first tug drove the great pine a quarter of its length into the earth.

"*A hw !*" shouted the Captain of the Little Black Ants, and Kahp-too-óo-yoo opened his eyes; but he could see nothing below.

"Shut your eyes again," said the Captain, giving the signal. Again the Little Black Ants pushed mightily against the sky, and the Big Red Ants pulled mightily from below; and the pine was driven another fourth of its length into the earth.

"*A hw !*" cried the Captain; and when Kahp-too-óo-yoo opened his eyes he could just see the big, brown world.

Again he closed his eyes. There was another great push and pull, and only a quarter of the pine was left above the ground. Now Kahp-too-óo-yoo could see, far below, the parched fields strewn with dead animals, and his own village full of dying people.

Again the Little Black Ants pushed and the Big Red Ants pulled, and this time the tree was driven clear out of sight, and Kahp-too-óo-yoo was left sitting on the ground. He hastily made a bow and arrows and soon killed a fat deer, which he brought and divided among the Little Black Ants and the Big Red Ants, thanking them for their kindness.

Then he made all his clothing to be new, for he had been four years à prisoner in the bewitched tree, and was all in rags. Making for himself a flute from the bark of a young tree, he played upon it as he strode homeward and sang :

Kahp-too-óo-yoo tú-mah-quee,
Nah-chóor kwé-shay-tin,
Nah-shúr kwé-shay-tin ;
Kahp-too-óo-yoo tú-mah-quee !

(Kahp-too-óo-yoo has come to life again,
Is back to his home coming,
Blowing the yellow and the blue;
Kahp-too-óo-yoo has come to life again!)

As he walked and sang, the forgotten clouds came over him, and the soft rain began to fall, and

all was green and good. But only so far as his voice reached came the rain; and beyond all was still death and drought. When he came to the end of the wet, he played and sang again; and again the rain fell as far as his voice was heard. This time the Fool-Boy, who was wandering outside the dying village, saw the far storm and heard the singing. He ran to tell Kahp-too-óo-yoo's parents; but nobody would believe a Foolish, and they sent him away.

When the Fool-Boy went out again, the rain fell on him and gave him strength, and he came running a second time to tell. Then the sisters came out of the house and saw the rain and heard the song;

ONE

KAHP-TOO-ÓO-YOO
CALLING THE RAIN.

and they cried for joy, and told their parents to rise and meet him. But the poor old people were dying of weakness, and could not rise; and the sisters went alone.   When they met him they fell on their knees, weeping; but Kahp-too-óo-yoo lifted them up and blessed them, gave an ear of blue corn to Blue-Corn-Maiden, and to Yellow-Corn-Maiden an ear of yellow corn, and brought them home.

As he sang again, the rain fell in the village; and when it touched the pinched faces of the dead they sat up and opened their mouths to catch it. And the dying crawled out to drink, and were strong again; and the withered fields grew green and glad.

When they came to the house, Kahp-too-óo-yoo blessed his parents, and then said:

"Little sisters, give us to eat."

But they answered, "How? For you have been gone these four years, and there was none to give us rain.   We planted, but nothing came, and to-day we ate the last grain."

"Nay, little sisters," he said. "A person should not think so.   Look now in the store-rooms, if there be not something there."

"But we have looked and looked, and turned over everything to try to find one grain."

"Yet look once more," he said; and when they opened the door, lo! there was the store-room piled to the roof with corn, and another room was full of wheat. Then they cried for joy, and began to roast the blue ears, for they were dying of hunger.

At the sweet smell of the roasting corn came the starving neighbors, crowding at the door, and crying:

"O Kahp-too-óo-yoo! Give us to taste one grain of corn, and then we will go home and die."

But Kahp-too-óo-yoo handed to each an ear, and said:

"Fathers, brothers, go now to your own houses, for there you will find corn as much as here." And when they went, it was so. All began to roast corn and to eat; and the dead in the houses awoke and were strong again, and all the village sang and danced.

From that time there was plenty of rain, for he who had the power of the clouds was at home again. In the spring the people planted, and in the fall the crops were so great that all the town could not hold them; so that which was left they brought to Shee-eh-whíb-bak (Isleta), where we enjoy it to this day.

As for the false friend, he died of shame in his house, not daring to come out; and no one wept for him.

XXIII

THE MAN WHO WOULD N'T KEEP SUNDAY

AMONG the folk-stories of the Pueblos which show at once that they are not of such antiquity as the rest, is this. It is plain that the story is post-Spanish—that it has been invented within the last three hundred and fifty years. That seems to us a long time to go back in the history of America, but to the Pueblos it is a trifling dot on the long line of their antiquity.

The following tale is an amusing instance of the fashion in which some of the myth-makers have mixed things. It is an Indian fairy tale, but with a Christian moral—which was learned from the noble and effective Spanish missionaries who toiled here.

Once upon a time, in a pueblo south of Isleta,— one of its old colonies known as P'ah-que-tóo-ai, the Rainbow Town, but deserted long ago,—there were two Indians who were great friends. They started in life with equal prospects, married young, and settled in the same town. But though friends, their natures were very different. One was a good man in his heart, and the other was bad. The good man always observed Sunday, but the other

worked every day. The good man had better luck
than the bad; and the latter became jealous. At
last he said: "Friend, tell me, why is it that you
always make more success than I?"

"Perhaps," answered Good, "because I keep
Sunday, but work hard all the other days of the
week, while you work every day."

Time went on, and both the friends accumu-
lated considerable wealth in servants, stock, and
ornaments. The good man let his servants rest
on Sunday, but the bad made his work every day,
and did not even give them time to smoke. Good
prospered most, and had more servants, more
stock, and more ornaments than Bad, who grew
more jealous daily. At last Bad said to Good:
"Friend, you say that you have good luck because
you keep Sunday, but I'll bet I am right in *not*
keeping it."

"No," replied Good; "I'll bet *I* am right, and
that Sunday ought to be kept."

"Then I will bet all my stock against all your
stock, and all my lands against your lands, and
everything we have except our wives. To-morrow, be ready about breakfast-time, and we will go
out into the public road and ask the first three
men we meet which of us is right. And whichever
gets the voice of the majority, he shall be the winner, and shall take all that is of the other."

Good agreed,—for an Indian cannot back out
of a challenge,—and so the next morning the two
friends took the public road. In a little while they
met a man, and said to him: "Friend, we want
your voice. Which of us is right, the one who

observes Sunday and lets his *peons* rest then, or he who does not?"

Now it happened that this person was not a man, but an old devil who was taking a walk in human form; and he promptly answered: "Without doubt he is right who does not keep Sunday," and went his road.

"Aha!" said Bad to Good. "You see I got the first voice."

They started on again and soon met another man, to whom they asked the same. But it was the same old devil, and he gave them the same answer.

"Aha!" said Bad. "Now I have the second voice, you see."

Presently they met a third man, and asked him the same, and he answered the same; for it was the same old devil in another body.

"Aha!" said Bad, "I am the winner! Get down from that burro, and let me have her and her colt, for now all that was yours is mine, as we agreed."

Good got down from the burro with tears in his eyes, for he was thinking of his wife, and said:

"Now, friend, having gained all, you are going back to our home; but I shall not. Tell my wife that I am going to the next pueblo to seek work, and that I will not be back until I have earned as much as I have lost in this bet, or more; but tell her not to be sad."

Then they shook hands and parted, Bad riding home full of joy, and Good trudging off through the sand toward Isleta, which was the largest and wealthiest pueblo of the tribe. On the road night

overtook him, and seeing an abandoned house in
a field, he hastened to it for shelter from the cold
of night. A portion of the roof still remained, with
the *fogon* (corner fireplace) and chimney, and he
began to brush a place to lie down. Now it happened that this house was the place where all the
devils of that country used to meet at night; and
before Good went to sleep he heard noises of the
devils coming. He was very much frightened, and
to hide himself climbed up into the chimney and
stood upon its crosspiece.

In a moment the devils began to arrive singly or
in pairs; and at last came the old devil — the very
one who had played the trick on Good. He called
the meeting to order, and asked them what they
had been doing. A young devil arose and said:

"The next pueblo is the largest and wealthiest
of this nation. For three weeks now, all its people,
and all the people along that river, have been
working at the spring from which the river comes,
but have not been able to undo me. Three weeks
ago I came to that spring and thought how nice it
would be to stop up the spring, and how the people
would swear if their gods did not send rain. So I
stuck a big stone in the spring and stopped all the
water; and ever since, the water will not come out,
and the people work in vain, and they are dying of
thirst, and all their stock. Now they will either
forsake their gods and serve us, or die like the
animals, thinking nothing of their past or future."

"Good!" said the old devil, rubbing his hands.
"You have done well! But tell me — is there no
way to open the spring?"

"There is only one way," said the young devil, "and one man could do that — but they will never think of it. If a man took a long stick, shaped like a sword, and went and stood on top of the stone, and struck it with the full length of the stick first east and west, and then north and south, the water would come out so hard that the stone would be thrown out upon the banks and the spring could never be stopped again."

"Is *that* the only way?" said the old devil. "You have done very well, for they certainly will never think to do that. Now for the next."

Then another young devil arose and reported this:

"I, too, have done something. In the pueblo across the mountain I have the daughter of the wealthiest man sick in bed, and she will never get well. All the medicine-men have tried in vain to cure her. She, too, will be ours."

"Good!" said the old devil. "But is there no way in which any one may cure her?"

"Yes, there is one way, but they never will think of that. If a person should carry her to the door just as the sun is rising, and hold her so that its very first rays would touch the top of her head, she would be well at once, and never could be made sick again."

"You are right," said the old devil, "they will never think of that. You have done well."

Just then a rooster crowed, and the old devil cried, "You have a road!"— which means, "an adjournment is in order." All the devils hurried away; and when they were gone, poor Good crawled down from the chimney half dead with fright, and hurried on toward Isleta. When he got there he found the people in great trouble, for their crops were withering and their cattle dying for want of water.

"I see," thought Good to himself, "that these devils told the truth about one thing, and so perhaps they did about all. I. will try to undo them, even if I fail." Going to the Cacique he asked what they would give him if he would open the spring. The Cacique told the *principales*, and they held a *junta*, and decided to let the stranger name his own price.

"Well," said he, "I will do this if you will give me half the value of the whole village."

They agreed, and asked how many men he would need to help him, and when he would begin.

"I need no men. Lend me only a hard stick the length of my outstretched arms, and a horse."

These were given him, and he went to the spring alone. Leaping upon the stone he struck it with the full length of the stick east and west, and then north and south, and sprang nimbly to the bank. At that very instant the water rushed out harder than it had ever done. All the people and cattle along the river came to the banks and drank and revived. They began to irrigate their fields again, and the dying crops grew green.[1] When Good got back to the pueblo, half of all the grain and money

---

[1] Here, as in several other stories in this volume, is a touch of the arid character of the Southwest. The country is always so dry that irrigation is necessary in farming, and in very bad years the streams have not water even for that. The Rio Grande itself frequently disappears in September between certain points in its course in sandy New Mexico; and within ten miles below Isleta I have seen its bed bone-dry. Ignorance of this fact has caused serious blunders on the part of historians unfamiliar with the country of which they wrote.

and dresses and ornaments were piled up in a huge pile waiting for him, and half the horses and cattle and sheep were waiting in big herds. It was so that he had to hire a great many men to help him home with his wealth, which was more than any one person ever had before. He appointed a mayordomo to take charge of this caravan, and to meet him at a certain point on the way home. He himself, taking a horse, rode away at once to the other pueblo, where the rich man's daughter was sick. Arriving at nightfall, he stopped at the house of an old woman. While he ate, she told him how sad was all the village; for the girl who had been so kind to all was dying.

"But," said he, "I can cure her."

"*In-dah*," said the crone; "for all the medicine-men have tried vainly, and how shall you?"

"But I can," he insisted; and at last the old woman went to the rich man, and said there was a stranger at her house who was sure he could cure the girl.

The *rico* said: "Go and tell him to come here quickly," and the old woman did so. When Good came, the rich man said: "Are you he who says he can cure my daughter?"

"I am the one."

"For how much will you cure her?"

"What will you give?"

"Half of all I have, which is much."

"It is well. To-morrow be ready, for I will come just before the sun."

In the blue of the morning Good came and waked the girl, and carried her to the door. In a

moment came the sun, and its first ray fell upon
her bent head. In an instant she was perfectly
well, and stronger and prettier than ever.

That very day her father gladly divided all his
wealth into two equal shares, and gave half to
Good, who again had to hire many cow-boys and
men with *carretas* to help him transport all this.
At the appointed spot he found his mayordomo;
and putting all the stock together, with many
herders, and all the wagons full of corn and dresses
and ornaments and money together, started homeward, sending ahead a messenger on a beautiful
horse to apprise his wife.

When the jealous Bad saw this fine horse going
to the house of his friend, he ran over to see what
it meant; and while he was still there, Good arrived with all his wealth. Filled with envy, Bad
asked him where he had got all this; and Good
told the whole story.

"Well," said Bad, "I will go there too, and perhaps I will hear something." So off he rode on the
burro he had won from Good, till he came to the
deserted house, and climbed up in the chimney.

Soon the devils met, and the two young ones
told their chief that the spring had been opened
and the girl cured, and that neither could ever be
bewitched again.

"Somebody must have listened to us last night,"
said the old devil, greatly troubled. "Search the
house." In a little while they found the jealous
friend in the chimney, and supposing him to be the
one who had undone them, without mercy puffed
him to the place where devils live.

XXIV

THE BRAVE BOBTAILS

WHEN it came old Anastacio's turn, one night, to tell a story to the waiting circle, it was several minutes before he responded to the quaint summons; and at last Lorenso repeated: "There is a tail to you, *compadre* Anastacio!" The words seemed to remind him of something; for he turned to his fat grandson, and said:

"Juan! Knowest thou why the Bear and the Badger have short tails? For once they had them long as Kéem-ee-deh, the Mountain Lion. *In-dah?* Then I will tell thee."

Once in the Days of the Old, it was that a young man lived here in Shee-eh-whíb-bak whom they called T'hoor-hlóh-ah, the Arrow of the Sun. He was not of thé Tée-wahn, but a Ute, who was taken in war while yet a child. When the warriors brought him here, a Grandmother who was very poor took him for her son, and reared him, loving him greatly, and teaching him all the works of men. Coming to be a young man, he was a mighty hunter; but so good in his heart that he loved the animals as brothers, and they all loved him. When he went out to hunt, the first game he killed he always dressed and left there for his animal-friends to eat. Sometimes it was Kéem-ee-deh, king of the four-feet, who came to the feast Sun-Arrow had made; and sometimes Kahr-naí-deh, the Badger, who is best of all to dig, and who showed Those of Old how to make their caves; and sometimes the smaller ones. They were all grateful; for no other was so kind to feed them.

Now the Grandmother would never let Sun-Arrow go to war, fearing that he would be killed; and all the other young men laughed at him, because he had never taken the sacred *oak-bark*. And when the others danced the great round-dance, he had to stand alone. So he was ashamed, and vowed that he would prove himself a man; and taking secretly his bow and arrows and his thunder-knife, he went away by night alone, and crossed the Eagle-Feather Mountains.

Now in that time there was always great war with the Comanches, who lived in the plains. They came often across the mountains and attacked Isleta by night, killing many people. Their chief was P'ee-kú-ee-fà-yíd-deh, or Red Scalp, the strongest and largest and bravest of men. For many years all the warriors of Isleta had tried to kill him, for he was the head of the war; but he slew all who came against him. He was very brave, and painted his scalp red with *páh-ree*, so that he might be known from far; and left his scalp-lock very long, and braided it neatly, so that an enemy might grasp it well.

Now Sun-Arrow met this great warrior; and

with the help of an old Spider-woman,[1] slew him
and took his scalp. When the people of Isleta
saw Sun-Arrow returning, the young men began to
laugh and say: "Va! T'hoor-hlóh-ah has gone to
make war again on the rabbits!'

But when he came into the plaza, saying nothing, and they saw that *oak-bark* which all knew,
all cried out: "Come and look! For here is Sun-
Arrow, who was laughed at — and now he has
brought the bark of Red Scalp, whom our bravest
have tried in vain to kill."

So when he had taken the scalp to the Cacique,
and they had had the round-dance, and the days
of purification were over, they called Sun-Arrow
the greatest warrior of the Tée-wahn, and made
him second to the Cacique. Then all who had
daughters looked at him with good eyes, and all
the maidens wished for so brave a husband. But
he saw none of them, except the youngest daughter
of the Cacique; for he loved her. When the Grandmother had spoken to the Cacique, and it was well,
they brought the young people together, and gave
them to eat of the betrothal corn — to Sun-Arrow
an ear of the blue corn, and to her an ear of the
white corn, because the hearts of maidens are
whiter than those of men. When both had eaten
the raw corn, every seed of it, the old folks said:
"It is well! For truly they love each other. And
now let them run the marrying-race."

Then all the people gathered yonder where are
the ashes of the evil-hearted ones who were burned
when Antelope Boy won for his people. And the

---

[1] About equivalent to our "fairy godmother."

elders marked a course, as of three miles, from there to the sacred sand-hill beside the Kú-mai. When they said the word, Sun-Arrow and the girl went running like young antelope, side by side. Up to the Place of the Bell they ran, and turned back running; and when they came to the people, the girl was a little in front, and all cried:

"It is well! For now Eé-eh-chah has won a husband, and she shall always be honored in her own house."

So they were married, and the Cacique blessed them. They made a house by the plaza,[1] and Sun-Arrow was given of the fields, that he might plant.

But of the maidens there was one who did not forgive Sun-Arrow that he would not look at her; and in her heart she thought to pay him. So she went to a Spider-woman,[2] and said: "Grand-mother, help me! For this young man despised me, and now I will punish him."

Then the Spider-woman made an accursed prayer-stick of the feathers of the woodpecker, and spoke to the Ghosts, and said to the girl:

"It is well, daughter! For I am the one that will help you. Take only this Toad, and bury it in your floor, *this* way, and then ask T'hoor-hlóh-ah to come to your house."

The girl made a hole in her floor, and buried P'ah-foo-ée-deh, the Toad. Then she went to Sun-Arrow and said: "Friend T'hoor-hlóh-ah, come to my house a little; for I have to talk to you."

But when Sun-Arrow sat down in her house, his

---

1 Public square in the center of the pueblo.
2 Here equivalent to a witch.

feet were upon the floor over the hole; and in a
moment the Toad grew very great, and began to
swallow him by the feet. Sun-Arrow kicked and
fought, for he was very strong. But he could do nothing; and in a little, he was swallowed to the knees.
Then he called in a great voice for his wife; and
all the people of the Tée-wahn came running with
her. When they saw him so, they were very sad;
and Eé-eh-çhah took his hand, and the Grandmother took his other, and all the people helped
them. But all were not so strong as the great
Toad; and fast it was swallowing him, until he was
at the waist. Then he said:

"Go, my people! Go, my wife! For it is in vain.
Go from this place, that you may not see me.
And pray to the Trues if they will help me." So
they all went, mourning greatly.

In that time it came that Shee-íd-deh, the
House-Mouse, stirred from his hole; and seeing
Sun-Arrow *so*, he came to him, weeping.

"Oh, Friend Sun-Arrow!" he cried. "You
who have been a father to us all, you who have fed
us, and have proved yourself so brave—it is not de-
served that you should be thus. But we for whom
you have cared, we will be the ones to help you!"

Then Shee-íd-deh ran from the house until he
found the Dog, and to him told it all. And Quee-
ah-níd-deh, whose voice was big, ran out into the
plains, up and down, *pregonando*[1] to all the animals; and they came hurrying from all places.
Soon all the birds and all the four-feet were met in

---

[1] The technical (Spanish) word for the official heralding by which all
announcements are still made among the Pueblos.

council in the room where Sun-Arrow was; and the Mountain Lion was captain. When he had listened to them, he said:

"Now let each tribe of you choose from it one who is young and strong, to give help to him who has fed us. For we cannot leave him to die so."

When every kind that walks or flies had chosen its strongest one, the chosen stood out; and Kéem-ee-deh called them by name to take their turns.

"Kóo-ah-raí-deh!" he called; and the Bluebird of the mountains came to Sun-Arrow, who was now swallowed up to his armpits. Sun-Arrow grasped her long tail with both hands, and she flew and flew with all her might, not caring for the pain, until her tail was pulled off. But Sun-Arrow was not budged a hair.

Then the captain called Ku-íd-deh, the Bear, to try. He gave his long tail to Sun-Arrow to hold; and when he had counted "One, two, *three!*" he pulled with a great pull, so hard that his whole tail came off. And still Sun-Arrow was not stirred.

Then it was to the Coyote. But *he* said: "My ears are stronger"; for he was a coward, and would not give to pull on his pretty tail, of which he is proud. So he gave to Sun-Arrow to hold by his ears, and began to pull backward. But soon it hurt him, and he stopped when his ears were pulled forward.

"Now it is to you, Kahr-naí-deh," said the Mountain Lion; and the Badger came out to try. First he dug around Sun-Arrow, and gave him to hold his tail. Then he counted *three*, and pulled greatly, so that his tail came off—and Sun-Arrow was moved a very little.   But the Badger did not fear the pain, and said:

"Let it be to me twice again, Kah-báy-deh."[1]

"It is well!" said the Mountain Lion.   "So let it be."

So the Badger dug again, and gave the stump of his tail, and pulled.   And Sun-Arrow was loosened a little more; but the stump slipped through his hands, for it was very short.

"*Around* me, friend," said the Badger, when he had dug a third time; and Sun-Arrow clasped his hands around the Badger's body, behind the fore legs.   Then for the third time Kahr-naí-deh pulled — so mightily that he dragged Sun-Arrow clear out from the Toad's mouth.   At that, all the animals fell upon the wicked Toad, and killed it; and gave thanks to Those Above for the deliverance of their friend.

When they had prayed, Sun-Arrow thanked all the animals, one by one; and to the Bluebird, the Bear, and the Badger, he said:

"Friends, how shall I thank you who have suffered so much for me? And how can I pay you for your help, and for the tails that you have lost?" But to the Coyote he did not say a word.

Then said the Badger:

"Friend T'hoor-hlóh-ah, as for me, your hand has always been held out to me.   You have fed me, and have been as a father: I want no pay for this tail that I have lost."

And the Bear and the Bluebird both answered the same thing.

1 Commander.

So Sun-Arrow again gave them many thanks, and they went away to their homes. As for Sun-Arrow, he hurried to the Medicine House, where all the Tée-wahn were making medicine[1] that he might be saved. And when they saw him entering, his wife ran and cried on his shoulder, and all the people gave thanks to the Trues.

Sun-Arrow told them all that was; and when the Father-of-all-Medicine looked in the sacred *cajete*[2] he saw the evil-hearted girl paying the Spider-woman. Then the Cum-pah-whít-la-wen[3] went running with their bows and arrows, and brought the girl; and she was punished as are they that have the evil road. As for the Spider-woman, she was already dead of shame; for she knew all that had been.

In a time it came that his father-in-law the Cacique died; and they made Sun-Arrow Cacique in his place. For many years he was so, bringing great good to his people; for he was very wise.

As for the Bear, the Badger, and the Bluebird, they would never go to the medicine-men of their tribes to have their tails mended to grow again; for they were proud that they had suffered to help their friend. And to this very day they go with short tails, and are honored by all the animals, and by all True Believers. But Too-wháy-deh, the

---

[1] Not compounding remedies, but going through the magic dance and incantations to which the Indians always resort in time of trouble. For a description of a medicine-making, see "Some Strange Corners of Our Country."

[2] A jar of magic water, in which the chief conjuror is supposed to see all that is going on in the world.

[3] Armed guards of the Medicine House.

coward, he who would not hurt himself with pulling
— he is a laughed-at to this day. For his ears
cannot lie back, as is well for beasts, but always
point straight forward, as Sun-Arrow pulled them.

Any one who has ever seen the Coyote, or any
other of the wolf or fox tribe, must have noticed
the alert forward pricking of the ears. Among the
Pueblos, any such peculiarity of nature—and particularly of animal life—is very sure to have a folk-
story hung to it. It has always seemed to me that
the boy who always wants to know "why?" has a
better time of it among my Indian friends than anywhere else. For there is always sure to be a why,
and an interesting one—which is much more satis-
factory than only learning that "it's bedtime now,"
or that "I'm busy."

THE REVENGE of the FAWNS

XXV

"DON CARLOS," said Vitorino, throwing another log upon the fire, which caught his tall shadow and twisted it and set it dancing against the rocky walls of the cañon in which we were camped for the night, "did you ever hear why the Wolf and the Deer are enemies?" And as he spoke he stretched out near me, looking up into my face to see if I were going to be interested.

A few years ago it would have frightened me very seriously to find myself thus — alone in one of the remotest corners of New Mexico save for that swarthy face peering up into mine by the weird light of the camp-fire. A stern, quiet but manly face it seems to me now; but once I would have

thought it a very savage one, with its frame of long,
jet hair, its piercing eyes, and the broad streak of
red paint across its cheeks. By this time, however, having lived long among the kindly Pueblos,
I had shaken off that strange, ignorant prejudice
against all that is unknown — which seems to be
inborn in all of us — and wondered that I could
ever have believed in that brutal maxim, worthy
only of worse than savages, that "A good Indian
is a dead Indian." For Indians are men, after all,
and astonishingly like the rest of us when one really
comes to know them.

I pricked up my ears — very glad at his hint of
another of these folk-stories.

"No," I answered. "I have noticed that the
Wolf and the Deer are not on good terms, but
never knew the reason."

"*Si, señor,*" said he,— for Vitorino knows no
English, and most of our talk was in Spanish, which
is easier to me than the Tée-wahn language,—
"that was very long ago, and now all is changed.
But once the Wolf and the Deer were like brothers;
and it is only because the Wolf did very wickedly
that they are enemies. *Con su licencia, señor.*"[1]

"*Bueno; anda!*"[2]

So Vitorino leaned his shoulders against a con-
venient rock and began.

Once upon a time, when the Wolf and the Deer
were friends, there were two neighbors in the country beyond the Rio Puerco, not far from where the

---

[1] "With your permission, sir."
[2] "All right; go ahead!"

pueblo of Laguna (a Quères town) now is. One
was a Deer-mother who had two fawns, and the
other a Wolf-mother with two cubs. They had
very good houses of adobe, just such as we live in
now, and lived like real people in every way. The
two were great friends, and neither thought of
going to the mountain for firewood or to dig
amole[1] without calling for the other to accompany
her.

One day the Wolf came to the house of the Deer
and said:

"Friend Peé-hlee-oh [Deer-woman], let us
go to-day for wood and amole, for I must wash
to-morrow."

"It is well, friend Káhr-hlee-oh," replied the
Deer. "I have nothing to do, and there is food
in the house for the children while I am gone.
Toó-kwai! [Let us go]."

So they went together across the plain and into
the hills till they came to their customary spot.
They gathered wood and tied it in bundles to bring
home on their backs, and dug amole, which they
put in their shawls to carry. Then the Wolf sat
down under a cedar-tree and said:

"Ai! But I am tired! Sit down, friend Deer-
woman, and lay your head in my lap, that we may
rest."

"No, I am not tired," replied the Deer.

"But just to rest a little," urged the Wolf. The
Deer good-naturedly lay down with her head in the
lap of her friend. But soon the Wolf bent down
and caught the trusting Deer by the throat, and

[1] The root of the palmilla, generally used for soap throughout the Southwest.

killed her.   That was the first time in the world that any one betrayed a friend, and from that deed comes all the treachery that is.

The false Wolf took off the hide of the Deer, and cut off some of the meat and carried it home on her load of *amole* and wood.   She stopped at the house of the Deer, and gave the Fawns some of the ac-cursed meat, saying:

"Friends, Deer-babies, do not fear, but eat; your mother met relatives and went to their house, and she will not come to-night."

The Fawns were very hungry, and as soon as the Wolf had gone home they built a big fire in the fireplace and set the meat to cook.   But at once it began to sputter and to hiss, and the Fawn who was tending it heard it cry, "Look out! look out! for this is your mother!"

He was greatly frightened, and called his brother to listen, and again the same words came from the meat.

"The wicked old Wolf has killed our *nana!* [mama]," they cried, and, pulling the meat from the fire, they laid it gently away and sobbed them-selves to sleep.

Next morning the Wolf went away to the mountain to bring the rest of the deer-meat; and when she was gone her Cubs came over to play with the Fawns, as they were used to doing. When they had played awhile, the Cubs said:

"*Pee-oo-wée-deh* [little Deer], why are you so prettily spotted, and why do you have your eye-lids red, while we are so ugly?"

"Oh," said the Fawns, "that is because when

16

we were little, like you, our mother put us in a room and smoked us, and made us spotted."

"Oh, Fawn-friends, can't you spot us, too, so that we may be pretty?"

So the Fawns, anxious to avenge the death of their mother, built a big fire of corn-cobs in the fireplace, and threw coyote-grass on it to make a great smoke. Then, shutting the Cubs into the room, they plastered up the door and windows with mud, and laid a flat rock on top of the chimney and sealed it around with mud; and climbing down from the roof, they took each other's hands and ran away to the south as fast as ever they could.

After they had gone a long way, they came to a Coyote. He was walking back and forth with one paw to his face, howling dreadfully with the tooth-ache. The Fawns said to him very politely:

"*Ah-bóo!* [poor thing]. Old-man friend, we are sorry your tooth hurts. But an old Wolf is chasing us, and we cannot stay. If she comes this way, asking about us, do not tell her, will you?"

"*Een-dah*. Little-Deer-friends, I will not tell her"—and he began to howl again with pain, while the Fawns ran on.

When the Wolf came to her home with the rest of the meat, the Cubs were not there; and she went over to the house of the Deer. It was all sealed and still; and when she pushed in the door, there were her Cubs dead in the smoke! When she saw that, the old Wolf was wild with rage, and vowed to follow the Fawns and eat them without mercy. She soon found their tracks leading away

THE WOLF, AND THE COYOTE WITH THE TOOTHACHE.

to the south, and began to run very swiftly in pursuit.

In a little while she came to the Coyote, who was still walking up and down, howling so that one could hear him a mile away. But not pitying his pain, she snarled at him roughly:

"Say, old man! have you seen two Fawns running away?"

The Coyote paid no attention to her, but kept walking with his hand to his mouth, groaning, "*Mm-m-páh! Mm-m-páh!*"

Again she asked him the same question, more snappishly, but he only howled and groaned. Then she was very angry, and showed her big teeth as she said:

"I don't care about your '*Mm-m-páh! Mm-m-páh!*' Tell me if you saw those Fawns, or I'll eat you this very now!"

"Fawns? *Fawns?*" groaned the Coyote — "I have been wandering with the toothache ever since the world began. And do you think I have had nothing to do but to watch for Fawns? Go along, and don't bother me."

So the Wolf, who was growing angrier all the time, went hunting around till she found the trail, and set to running on it as fast as she could go.

By this time the Fawns had come to where two Indian boys were playing *k'wah-t'hím* [1] with their bows and arrows, and said to them:

"Friends boys, if an old Wolf comes along and asks if you have seen us, don't tell her, will you?"

The boys promised that they would not, and the

---

[1] A sort of walking archery.

Fawns hurried on. But the Wolf could run much faster, and soon she came to the boys, to whom she cried gruffly:

"You boys! did you see two Fawns running this way?"

But the boys paid no attention to her, and went on playing their game and disputing: "My arrow's nearest!" "No; mine is!" "'T ain't! Mine is!" She repeated her question again and again, but got no answer till she cried in a rage:

"You little rascals! Answer me about those Fawns, or I'll eat you!"

At that the boys turned around and said:

"We have been here all day, playing *k'wah-t'hím*, and not hunting Fawns. Go on, and do not disturb us."

So the Wolf lost much time with her questions and with finding the trail again; but then she began to run harder than ever.

In the mean time the Fawns had come to the bank of the Rio Grande, and there was *P'ah-chah-hlóo-hlí*, the Beaver, hard at work cutting down a tree with his big teeth. And they said to him very politely:

"Friend Old-Crosser-of-the-Water, will you please pass us over the river?"

The Beaver took them on his back and carried them safely across to the other bank. When they had thanked him, they asked him not to tell the old Wolf about them. He promised he would not, and swam back to his work. The Fawns ran and ran, across the plain, till they came to a big black hill of lava that stands alone in the valley southeast of Tomé.

THE WOLF MEETS THE BOYS PLAYING WITH THEIR BOWS AND ARROWS.

"Here!" said one of the Fawns, "I am sure this must be the place our mother told us about, where the Trues of our people live.   Let us look."

And when they came to the top of the hill, they found a trap-door in the solid rock.   When they knocked, the door was opened and a voice called, "Enter!" They went down the ladder into a great room underground; and there they found all the Trues of the Deer-people, who welcomed them and gave them food.

When they had told their story, the Trues said: "Fear not, friends, for we will take care of you."

And the War-captain picked out fifty strong young bucks for a guard.

By this time the Wolf had come to the river, and there she found the Beaver hard at work and grunting as he cut the tree.

"Old man!" she snarled, "did you see two Fawns here?"

But the Beaver did not notice her, and kept on walking around the tree, cutting it and grunting, "*Ah-oó-mah! Ah-oó-mah!*"

She was in a terrible rage now, and roared:

"I am not talking '*Ah-oó-mah!*' to you.   I'm asking if you saw two Fawns."

"Well," said the Beaver, "I have been cutting trees here by the river ever since I was born, and I have no time to think about Fawns."

The Wolf, crazy with rage, ran up and down the bank, and at last came back and said:

"Old man, if you will carry me over the river I will pay you; but if you don't, I'll eat you up."

"Well, wait then till I cut around the tree three

times more," said the Beaver; and he made her
wait. Then he jumped down in the water and
took her on his neck, and began to swim across.
But as soon as he came where the water was deep,
he dived to the bottom and stayed there as long as
he could.

"Ah-h-h!" sputtered the Wolf when he came to
the surface. As soon as the Beaver got a breath,
down he went again; and so he kept doing all the
way across, until the Wolf was nearly drowned —
but she clung to his neck desperately, and he could
not shake her off.

When they came to the shore the old Wolf was
choking, coughing, and crying, and so mad that
she would not pay the Beaver as she had promised
— and from that day to this the Beaver will never
again ferry a Wolf across the river.

Presently she found the trail, and came running
to the hill. When she knocked on the trap-door a
voice from within called, "Who?"

"Wolf-woman," she answered as politely as she
could, restraining her anger.

"Come down," said the voice, and hearing her
name the fifty young Deer-warriors — who had
carefully whetted their horns — stood ready. The
door flew open, and she started down the ladder.
But as soon as she set her foot on the first rung,
all the Deer-people shouted:

"Look what feet!" For, though the Deer is so
much larger than the Wolf, it has smaller feet.

At this she was very much ashamed, and pulled
back her foot; but soon her anger was stronger,
and she started down again. But each time the

"THE FAWNS APPEARED SUDDENLY, AND AT SIGHT OF THEM THE WOLF DROPPED THE SPOONFUL OF SOUP."

Deer-people laughed and shouted, and she drew back.

At last they were quiet, and she came down the ladder. When she had told her story the old men of the Deer-people said :

"This is a serious case, and we must not judge it lightly. Come, we will make an agreement. Let soup be brought, and we will eat together. And if you eat all your soup without spilling a drop, you shall have the Fawns."

"Ho!" thought the Wolf. "*That* is easy enough, for I will be very careful." And aloud she said: "It is well. Let us eat."

So a big bowl of soup was brought, and each took a *guayave* [1] and rolled it like a spoon to dip up the soup. The old Wolf was very careful, and had almost finished her soup without spilling a drop. But just as she was lifting the last sup to her mouth the Fawns appeared suddenly in the door of the next room, and at sight of them she dropped the soup in her lap.

"She spilled!" shouted all the Deer-people, and the fifty chosen warriors rushed upon her and tore her to pieces with their sharp horns.

That was the end of the treacherous Wolf; and from that day the Wolf and the Deer have been enemies, and the Wolf is a little afraid of the Deer. And the two Fawns? Oh, they still live with the Deer-people in that black hill below Tomé.

---

[1] An Indian bread made by spreading successive films of blue corn-meal batter on a flat hot stone. It looks more like a piece of wasp's nest than anything else, but is very good to eat.

XXVI

ANOTHER folk-story told by the Quères colony in Isleta also relates to Acoma, perched
upon the great round cliff in its far, fair valley.

Among the folk-lore heroes of whom every
Quères lad has heard is Ees-tée-ah Muts, the Arrow Boy. He was a great hunter and did many
remarkable things, but there was once a time when
all his courage and strength were of no avail,—
when but for the help of a little squirrel he would
have perished miserably.

On reaching manhood Ees-tée-ah Muts married
the daughter of the Kot-chin (chief). She was a
very beautiful girl and her hunter-husband was
very fond of her. But, alas! she was secretly a
witch and every night when Ees-tée-ah Muts was
asleep she used to fly away to the mountains,
where the witches held their uncanny meetings.
You must know that these witches have dreadful
appetites, and that there is nothing in the world
of which they are so fond as boiled baby.

Ees-tée-ah Muts, who was a very good man,
had no suspicion that his wife was guilty of such

practices, and she was very careful to keep him in ignorance of it.

One day, when the witch-wife was planning to go to a meeting, she stole a fat young baby and put it to cook in a great *olla* (earthen jar) in the dark inner room.   But before night she found she must go for water, and as the strange stone reservoir at Acoma is a laborious half-mile from the houses, she would be gone some time.   So, as she departed with a bright-painted *tinaja* upon her head, she charged her husband on no account to enter the inner room.

When she was gone Ees-tée-ah Muts began to ponder what she had said, and he feared that all was not well.   He went to the inner room and looked around, and when he found the baby cooking he was grieved, as any good husband would be, for then he knew that his wife was a witch. But when his wife returned with water, he said not a word, keeping only a sharp lookout to see what would come.

Very early that night Ees-tée-ah Muts pretended to go to sleep, but he was really very wide awake. His wife was quiet, but he could feel that she was watching him.   Presently a cat came sneaking into the room and whispered to the witch-wife:

"Why do you not come to the meeting, for we await you?"

"Wait me yet a little," she whispered, "until the man is sound asleep."

The cat crept away, and Ees-tée-ah Muts kept very still.   By and by an owl came in and bade the woman hurry.   And at last, thinking her hus-

band asleep, the witch-wife rose noiselessly and
went out. As soon as she was gone, Ees-tée-ah
Muts got up and followed her at a distance, for it
was a night of the full moon.

The witch-wife walked a long way till she came
to the foot of the Black Mesa, where was a great
dark hole with a rainbow in its mouth. As she
passed under the rainbow she turned herself into a
cat and disappeared within the cave. Ees-tée-ah
Muts crept softly up and peered in. He saw a
great firelit room full of witches in the shapes of
ravens and vultures, wolves and other animals of ill
omen. They were gathered about their feast and
were enjoying themselves greatly, eating and dancing and singing and planning evil to mankind.

For a long time Ees-tée-ah Muts watched them,
but at last one caught sight of his face peering in
at the hole.

"Bring him in!" shouted the chief witch, and
many of them rushed out and surrounded him and
dragged him into the cave.

"Now," said the chief witch, who was very angry,
"we have caught you as a spy and we ought to kill
you. But if you will save your life and be one
of us, go home and bring me the hearts of your
mother and sister, and I will teach you all our ways,
so that you shall be a mighty wizard."

Ees-tée-ah Muts hurried home to Acoma and
killed two sheep; for he knew, as every Indian
knows, that it was useless to try to escape from the
witches. Taking the hearts of the sheep, he
quickly returned to the chief witch, to whom he
gave them. But when the chief witch pricked the
hearts with a sharp stick they swelled themselves

out like a frog.   Then he knew that he had been
deceived, and was very angry, but pretending not
to care he ordered Ees-tée-ah Muts to go home,
which the frightened hunter was very glad to do.

But next morning when Ees-tée-ah Muts awoke
he was not in his own home at all, but lying on a
tiny shelf far up a dizzy cliff.   To jump was certain
death, for it was a thousand feet to the ground;
and climb he could not, for the smooth rock rose a
thousand feet above his head.   Then he knew that
he had been bewitched by the chief of those that
have the evil road, and that he must die.   He
could hardly move without falling from the narrow
shelf, and there he lay with bitter thoughts until
the sun was high overhead.

At last a young Squirrel came running along
the ledge, and, seeing him, ran back to its mother,
crying:

"*Nana! Nana!*   Here is a dead man lying
on our ledge!"

"No, he is not dead," said the Squirrel-mother
when she had looked, "but I think he is very
hungry.   Here, take this acorn-cup and carry him
some corn-meal and water."

The young Squirrel brought the acorn-cup full
of wet corn-meal, but Ees-tée-ah Muts would not
take it, for he thought:

"Pah! What is so little when I am fainting
for food?"

But the Squirrel-mother, knowing what was in
his heart, said:

"Not so, *Sau-kée-ne* [friend].   It looks to be
little, but there will be more than enough.   Eat
and be strong."

Still doubting, Ees-tée-ah Muts took the cup
and ate of the blue corn-meal until he could eat no
longer, and yet the acorn-cup was not empty.
Then the young Squirrel took the cup and brought
it full of water, and though he was very thirsty he
could not drain it.

"Now, friend," said the Squirrel-mother, when
he was refreshed by his meal, "you cannot yet
get down from here, where the witches put you;
but wait, for I am the one that will help you."

She went to her store-room and brought out a
pine-cone, which she dropped over the great cliff.
Ees-tée-ah Muts lay on the narrow ledge as
patiently as he could, sleeping sometimes and
sometimes thinking of his strange plight. Next
morning he could see a stout young pine-tree
growing at the bottom of the cliff, where he was
very sure there had been no tree at all the day
before. Before night it was a large tree, and the
second morning it was twice as tall. The young
Squirrel brought him meal and water in the acorn-
cup twice a day, and now he began to be confident
that he would escape.

By the evening of the fourth day the magic pine
towered far above his head, and it was so close to
the cliff that he could touch it from his shelf.

"Now, Friend Man," said the Squirrel-mother,
"follow me!" and she leaped lightly into the tree.
Ees-tée-ah Muts seized a branch and swung over
into the tree, and letting himself down from bough
to bough, at last reached the ground in safety.

The Squirrel-mother came with him to the
ground, and he thanked her for her kindness.

"But now I must go back to my home," she said. "Take these seeds of the pine-tree and these piñon-nuts which I have brought for you, and be very careful of them. When you get home, give your wife the pine-seeds, but you must eat the piñons. So now, good-by," and off she went up the tree.

When Ees-tée-ah Muts had come to Acoma and climbed the dizzy stone ladder and stood in the adobe town, he was very much surprised. For the four days of his absence had really been four years, and the people looked strange. All had given him up for dead, and his witch-wife had married another man, but still lived in the same house, which was hers.[1] When Ees-tée-ah Muts entered she seemed very glad to see him, and pretended to know nothing of what had befallen him. He said nothing about it, but talked pleasantly while he munched the piñon-nuts, giving her the pine-seeds to eat. Her new husband made a bed for Ees-tée-ah Muts, and in the morning very early the two men went away together on a hunt.

That afternoon the mother of the witch-wife went to visit her daughter, but when she came near the house she stopped in terror, for far up through the roof grew a great pine-tree, whose furry arms came out at doors and windows. That was the end of the witch-wife, for the magic seed had sprouted in her stomach, and she was turned into a great, sad Pine that swayed above her home, and moaned and sobbed forever, as all her Pine-children do to this day.

[1] It is one of the fundamental customs of the Pueblos that the house and its general contents belong to the wife; the fields and other outside property to the husband.

XXVII

THE QUÈRES DIANA

THERE is a fragmentary Quères folk-story which bears internal evidence that its heroine was the mother of the Hero Twins—that is, the Moon. The adventure described here is one of those which befell the Moon-Mother, as related in several myths; though it has been varied, evidently by some later story-teller, and the identity of the heroine does not appear at first sight. It is a story common to all the Quères, and is undoubtedly ancient; but as I heard it first in Isleta its scene is laid in Laguna, a pueblo only two hundred years old.

Once upon a time the Tah-póh-pee[1] of Laguna had a daughter, who was the belle of the village. She was very fond of hunting, and killed as much game as any of the young men. Several miles south of Laguna is a very large sandstone dome rising in the plain, and in the heart of this rock the Governor's daughter had hollowed out a room in which she used to camp when on her hunting-expeditions.

One day there came a snow that covered the

[1] Governor.

ground so that one could easily track rabbits, and
taking her bow and arrows she started off to hunt.

She had unusual luck, and by the time she
reached the hunting-lodge she was loaded down
with rabbits. The evening was very cold, and she
was hungry; so, going into the rock-house, she
built a fire on the hearth and began to roast a rabbit. Just as it was cooking a strong west wind
came up and carried the savory smell from her
chimney far to the east, till it reached a dark cav-
ern in the Sandia Mountains, fifty miles away.
There lived an old giantess, the terror of all the
world, and when she caught a whiff of that sweet
meat she started up and rubbed her big red eye.

"Um!" she cried, "that is good! I am going to see
where it is, for I have had nothing to eat to-day."

In two steps she was at the rock-house, and,
stooping down, she called at the door: "Quáh-
tzee? [How are you?] What are you cooking in
there?"

"Rabbits," said the girl, dreadfully scared at
that great voice.

"Then give me one," shouted the old giantess.
The girl threw one out at the door, and the
giantess swallowed it at a gulp and demanded
more. The girl kept throwing them out until all
were gone. Then the giantess called for her
manta (dress), and her shawl and her buckskin
leggings, and ate them all, and at last said:

"Little girl, now you come out, and let me eat
you."

The girl began to cry bitterly when she saw that
great savage eye at the door, which was so small

that the giantess could not get her huge hand in. She repeated her commands thrice, and when the girl still refused to come out, picked up a great boulder and began to hammer the rock-house to pieces.   But just as she had broken off the roof and stooped to pick out the girl, two hunters chanced to pass and hear the noise.   They crept up and shot the giantess through the neck with their strong arrows and killed her, and, bringing new clothes for the girl, took her home safely to Kó-iks (the native name for Laguna), where she lived for many years.

XXVIII

A PUEBLO BLUEBEARD

ANOTHER fragmentary story of the Quères seems to refer to this same remarkable woman. You will see the connection when you remember that the Moon disappears every month; and I should judge that the following myth means that the Storm-King steals her.

Once upon a time a chief of Acoma had a lovely daughter. One day a handsome stranger stole her and took her away to his home, which was in the heart of the Snow Mountain (Mt. San Mateo). He was none other than Mast-Truan, one of the Storm-Gods. Bringing his captive home, the powerful stranger gave her the finest clothing and treated her very nicely. But most of the time he had to be away from home, attending to the storms, and she became very lonesome, for there was no one to keep her company but Mast-Truan's wrinkled old mother.

One day when she could stand the loneliness no longer, she decided to take a walk through the enormous house and look at the rooms which she had not seen. Opening a door she came into a very large room toward the east; and there were a lot of women crying and shivering with cold, for they had nothing to wear. Going through this room she came to another, which was full of gaunt, starving women, and here and there one lay dead upon the floor; and in the next room were scores of bleached and ghastly skeletons. And this was what Mast-Truan did with his wives when he was tired of them. The girl saw her fate, and, returning to her room, sat down and wept—but there was no escape, for Mast-Truan's old hag of a mother forever guarded the outer door.

When Mast-Truan came home again, his wife said: "It is now long that I have not seen my fathers. Let me go home for a little while."

"Well," said he, "here is some corn which must be shelled. When you have shelled it and ground it, I will let you out"; and he showed her four great rooms piled from floor to ceiling with ears of corn. It was more than one could shell in a year; and when her husband went out, she sat down again to cry and bemoan her fate.

Just then a queer little old woman appeared before her, with a kindly smile. It was a *cumúsh-quio* (fairy-woman).

"What is the matter, my daughter?" asked the old fairy, gently, "and why do you weep?"

The captive told her all, and the fairy said: "Do not fear, daughter, for I will help you, and we will have all the corn shelled and ground in four days."

So they fell to work. For two days the girl kept shelling; and though she could not see the old fairy at all, she could always hear at her side the click of the ears together. Then for two days she kept grinding on her *metate*, apparently alone, but hearing the constant grind of another *metate* close beside her. At the end of the fourth day the last kernel had been scrubbed into blue meal, and she was very happy. Then the old fairy-woman appeared again, bringing a large basket and a rope. She opened the doors to all the rooms where the poor women were prisoners, and bade them all get into the basket one by one. Mast-Truan had taken away the ladder from the house when he left, that no one might be able to get out; but with her basket and rope the good old fairy-woman let them all down to the ground, and told them to hurry home—which they did as fast as ever their poor, starved legs could carry them. Then the fairy-woman and the girl escaped, and made their way to Acoma. So there was a Moon again—and that it *was* the Moon, we may be very sure; since this same girl became the mother of the Hero Twins, who were assuredly Children of the Moon.

XXIX

THE HERO TWINS

THAT the heroes of "The Magic Hide-and-Seek" were really the Pueblo Castor and Pollux, the twin offspring of the Sun-Father and the Moon-Mother, is more than probable. For some reason which I do not know, these demigods do not figure as clearly in the Tée-wahn myths as among the other Pueblos, the Navajos and the Apaches; but that they are believed in, even in Isleta, there can be no doubt. They were the ones who led mankind forth from its first home in the dark center of the earth.[1] The rainbow is their bow, the lightnings are their arrows. Among the other Pueblos there are countless folk-stories about these Hero Twins; and the following example myth will quickly remind you of the boys who played hide-and-seek. It is told in Isleta, though I have never heard it from the Tée-wahn people there. Ever since the great drouth of a generation ago, about one hundred and fifty Quères, starved out from the pueblos of Acoma and La-guna, have dwelt in Isleta, and they are now a

---

[1] They are represented in the sacred dances by the Káh-pee-óo-nin, "the Dying-of-Cold" (because they are always naked except for the breech-clout).

permanent part of the village, recognized by rep-
resentation in the civil and religious government,
though speaking an altogether different language.
Tée-wahn and Quères cannot understand each
other in their own tongues, so they have to com-
municate in Spanish.

Máw-Sahv and Oó-yah-wee, as the Hero Twins
are named in Quères, had the Sun for a father.
Their mother died when they were born, and lay
lifeless upon the hot plain. But the two wonderful
boys, as soon as they were a minute old, were big
and strong, and began playing.

There chanced to be in a cliff to the southward a
nest of white crows; and presently the young crows
said: "*Nana*, what is that over there? Is n't it
two babies?"

"Yes," replied the Mother-Crow, when she had
taken a look. "Wait and I will bring them." So
she brought the boys safely, and then their dead
mother; and, rubbing a magic herb on the body
of the latter, soon brought her to life.

By this time Máw-Sahv and Oó-yah-wee were
sizable boys, and the mother started homeward
with them.

"Now," said she when they reached the edge of
the valley and could look across to that wondrous
rock whereon stands Acoma, "go to yonder town, .
my sons, for that is Ah-ko, where live your grandfather and grandmother, my parents; and I will
wait here. Go ye in at the west end of the town
and stand at the south end of the council-grounds
until some one speaks to you; and ask them to
take you to the Cacique, for he is your grandfather.

You will know his house, for the ladder to it has three uprights instead of two. When you go in and tell your story, he will ask you a question to see if you are really his grandchildren, and will give you four chances to answer what he has in a bag in the corner. No one has ever been able to guess what is in it, but there are birds."

The Twins did as they were bidden, and presently came to Acoma and found the house of the old Cacique. When they entered and told their story, he said: "Now I will try you. What is in yonder bag?"

"A rattlesnake," said the boys.

"No," said the Cacique, "it is not a rattlesnake. Try again."

"Birds," said the boys.

"Yes, they are birds. Now I know that you are truly my grandchildren, for no one else could ever guess." And he welcomed them gladly, and sent them back with new dresses and jewelry to bring their mother.

When she was about to arrive, the Twins ran ahead to the house and told her father, mother, and sister to leave the house until she should enter; but not knowing what was to come, they would not go out. When she had climbed the big ladder to the roof and started down through the trap-door by the room-ladder, her sister cried out with joy at seeing her, and she was so startled that she fell from the ladder and broke her neck, and never could be brought to life again.

Máw-Sahv and Oó-yah-wee grew up to astounding adventures and achievements. While still very young in years, they did very remarkable things; for they had a miraculously rapid growth, and at an age when other boys were toddling about home, these Hero Twins had already become very famous hunters and warriors. They were very fond of stories of adventure, like less precocious lads; and after the death of their mother they kept their grandmother busy telling them strange tales. She had a great many anecdotes of a certain ogre-giantess who lived in the dark gorges of the mountains to the South, and so much did Máw-Sahv and Oó-yah-wee hear of this wonderful personage — who was the terror of all that country — that their boyish ambition was fired.

One day when their grandmother was busy they stole away from home with their bows and arrows, and walked miles and miles, till they came to a great forest at the foot of the mountain. In the edge of it sat the old Giant-woman, dozing in the sun, with a huge basket beside her. She was so enormous and looked so fierce that the boys' hearts stood still, and they would have hidden, but just then she caught sight of them, and called: "Come, little boys, and get into this basket of mine, and I will take you to my house."

"Very well," said Máw-Sahv, bravely hiding his alarm. "If you will take us through this big forest, which we would like to see, we will go with you."

The Giant-woman promised, and the lads clambered into her basket, which she took upon her back and started off. As she passed through the woods, the boys grabbed lumps of pitch from the

tall pines and smeared it all over her head and
back so softly that she did not notice it. Once she
sat down to rest, and the boys slyly put a lot of big
stones in the basket, set fire to her pitched hair,
and hurriedly climbed a tall pine.

Presently the Giant-woman got up and started
on toward home; but in a minute or two her head
and *manta* were all of a blaze. With a howl that
shook the earth, she dropped the basket and rolled
on the ground, grinding her great head into the
sand until she at last got the fire extinguished.
But she was badly scorched and very angry, and
still angrier when she looked in the basket and
found only a lot of stones. She retraced her steps
until she found the boys hidden in the pine-tree,
and said to them: "Come down, children, and get
into my basket, that I may take you to my house,
for now we are almost there."

The boys, knowing that she could easily break
down the tree if they refused, came down. They
got into the basket, and soon she brought them to
her home in the mountain. She set them down
upon the ground and said: "Now, boys, go and
bring me a lot of wood, that I may make a fire in
the oven and bake you some sweet cakes."

The boys gathered a big pile of wood, with
which she built a roaring fire in the adobe oven
outside the house. Then she took them and
washed them very carefully, and taking them by
the necks, thrust them into the glowing oven and
sealed the door with a great, flat rock, and left
them there· to be roasted.

But the Trues were friends of the Hero Twins,

and did not let the heat harm them at all. When the old Giant-woman had gone into the house, Máw-Sahv and Oó-yah-wee broke the smaller stone that closed the smoke-hole of the oven, and crawled out from their fiery prison unsinged. They ran around and caught snakes and toads and gathered up dirt and dropped them down into the oven through the smoke-hole; and then, watching when the Giant-woman's back was turned, they sneaked into the house and hid in a huge *olla* on the shelf.

Very early in the morning the Giant-woman's baby began to cry for some boy-meat. "Wait till it is well cooked," said the mother; and hushed the child till the sun was well up. Then she went out and unsealed the oven, and brought in the sad mess the boys had put there. "They have cooked away to almost nothing," she said; and she and the Giant-baby sat down to eat. "Is n't this nice?" said the baby; and Máw-Sahv could not help saying, "You nasty things, to like that!"

"Eh? Who is that?" cried the Giant-woman, looking around till she found the boys hidden in the *olla*. So she told them to come down, and gave them some sweet cakes, and then sent them out to bring her some more wood.

It was evening when they returned with a big load of wood, which Máw-Sahv had taken pains to get green. He had also picked up in the mountains a long, sharp splinter of quartz.[1] The evening was cool, and they built a big fire in the fireplace. But immediately, as the boys had planned,

---

[1] A thunder-knife.

the green wood began to smoke at a dreadful rate, and soon the room was so dense with it that they all began to cough and strangle. The Giant-woman got up and opened the window and put her head out for a breath of fresh air; and Máw-Sahv, pulling out the white-hot splinter of quartz from the fire, stabbed her in the back so that she died. Then they killed the Giant-baby, and at last felt that they were safe.

Now the Giant-woman's house was a very large one, and ran far back into the very heart of the mountain. Having got rid of their enemies, the Hero Twins decided to explore the house; and, taking their bows and arrows, started boldly down into the deep, dark rooms. After traveling a long way in the dark, they came to a huge room in which corn and melons and pumpkins were growing abundantly. On and on they went, till at last they heard the growl of distant thunder. Following the sound, they came presently to a room in the solid rock, wherein the lightning was stored. Going in, they took the lightning and played with it awhile, throwing it from one to the other, and at last started home, carrying their strange toy with them.

When they reached Acoma and told their grandmother of their wonderful adventures, she held up her withered old hands in amazement. And she was nearly scared to death when they began to play with the lightning, throwing it around the house as though it had been a harmless ball, while the thunder rumbled till it shook the great rock of Acoma. They had the blue lightning which belongs in the West; and the yellow lightning of the

North; and the red lightning of the East; and the white lightning of the South; and with all these they played merrily.

But it was not very long till Shée-wo-nah, the Storm-King, had occasion to use the lightning; and when he looked in the room where he was wont to keep it, and found it gone, his wrath knew no bounds. He started out to find who had stolen it; and passing by Acoma he heard the thunder as the Hero Twins were playing ball with the lightning. He pounded on the door and ordered them to give him his lightning, but the boys refused. Then he summoned the storm, and it began to rain and blow fearfully outside; while within the boys rattled their thunder in loud defiance, regardless of their grandmother's entreaties to give the Storm-King his lightning.

It kept raining violently, however, and the water came pouring down the chimney until the room was nearly full, and they were in great danger of drowning. But luckily for them, the Trues were still mindful of them; and just in the nick of time sent their servant, Teé-oh-pee, the Badger, who is the best of diggers, to dig a hole up through the floor; all the water ran out, and they were saved. And so the Hero Twins outwitted the Storm-King.

South of Acoma, in the pine-clad gorges and mesas, the world was full of Bears. There was one old She-Bear in particular, so huge and fierce that all men feared her; and not even the boldest hunter dared go to the south—for there she had her home with her two sons.

Máw-sahv and Oó-yah-wee were famous hunters, and always wished to go south; but their
grandmother always forbade them. One day,
however, they stole away from the house, and got
into the cañon. At last they came to the She-
Bear's house; and there was old Quée-ah asleep
in front of the door. Máw-sahv crept up very
carefully and threw in her face a lot of ground
chile,[1] and ran. At that the She-Bear began to
sneeze, *ah-hútch! ah-hútch!* She could not stop,
and kept making *ah-hútch* until she sneezed herself to death.

Then the Twins took their thunder-knives and
skinned her. They stuffed the great hide with
grass, so that it looked like a Bear again, and tied
a buckskin rope around its neck.

"Now," said Máw-sahv, "We will give our
grandma a trick!"

So, taking hold of the rope, they ran toward
Acoma, and the Bear came behind them as if leaping. Their grandmother was going for water;
and from the top of the cliff she saw them running
so in the valley, and the Bear jumping behind
them. She ran to her house and painted one side
of her face black with charcoal, and the other side
red with the blood of an animal;[2] and, taking a bag
of ashes, ran down the cliff and out at the Bear, to
make it leave the boys and come after her.

But when she saw the trick, she reproved the
boys for their rashness — but in her heart she was
very proud of them.

---

[1] The fiery red-pepper of the Southwest.
[2] Ancient tokens of mourning.

XXX

A DISOBEDIENT child is something I have never seen among the Pueblos, in all the years I have lived with them. The parents are very kind, too. My little *amigos* in Isleta and the other Pueblo towns — for they are my friends in all — are never spoiled ; but neither are they punished much.[1] Personal acquaintance with a spanking is what very few of them have. The idea of obedience is inborn and inbred. A word is generally enough ; and for extreme cases it only needs the threat: " Look out, or I will send for the Grandfathers ! "

Now, perhaps you do not know who the Grandfathers are ; but every Pueblo youngster does. It has nothing to do with the " truly " grandpa, who is as lovely an institution among the Tée-wahn as anywhere else. No, the *Abuelos* were of an altogether different sort. That name is Spanish, and has three applications in Isleta: real grandparents ; the remarkable masked officials of a certain dance ; and the bad Old Ones. These last

---

[1] I must qualify this now. In the last two years I have seen one spoiled child — just one, in ten years' acquaintance with 9000 Pueblos !

are called in the Tée-wahn tongue *T'ai-kár-nin*
(Those-Who-Eat-People). They were, in fact, aboriginal Ogres, who once sadly ravaged Isleta.

The *T'ai-kár-nin* had no town, but dwelt in
caves of the lava mountain a couple of miles west
of this village — the *Kú-mai* hill. It is a bad
place at best: bleak, black, rough, and forbidding
— just the place that a properly constituted Ogre
would choose for his habitation. In the first place,
it is to the west of the town, which is "bad medicine" in itself to any Indian, for that point of the
compass belongs to the dead and to bad spirits.
Then its color is against it; and, still worse, it is to
this day the common stamping-ground of all the
witches in this part of the country, where they
gather at night for their diabolical caucuses. Of
its serious disrepute I can convey no better idea
to the enlightened and superstitionless American
mind than by saying that it is a sort of aboriginal
"haunted house."

So the hill of *Kú-mai* was a peculiarly fit place
for the Ogres to dwell in. Deep in its gloomy
bowels they huddled on the white sand which floors
all the caves there; and crannies overhead carried
away the smoke from their fires, which curled from
crevices at the top of the peak far above them.
Ignorant Americans would probably have taken it
for a volcanic emission; but the good people of
Shee-eh-whíb-bak knew better.

These Ogres were larger than ordinary men,
but otherwise carried no outward sign of their odi-
ous calling. Their teeth were just like anybody's
good teeth, and they had neither "tushes" nor

horns nor hoofs. Indeed, except for their unusual size, they would have been easily mistaken for Indians of some distant tribe. But, *ay de mi!* How strong they were! One could easily whip five common men in a bunch—"men even as strong as my son, Francisco," says Desiderio; and Francisco is as stout as a horse.

They were people of very fastidious palates, these Ogres. Nothing was good enough for them except human flesh—and young at that. Their fare was entirely baby—baby young, baby brown, and baby very fat. They never molested the adults; but as often as they found an appetite they descended upon the village, scooped up what children they could lay their hands upon, and carried them off to their caves. There they had enormous *ollas*, into which half a dozen children could be thrown at once.

There seemed to be some spell about these Ogres—besides their frequent hungry spells—for the Pueblos, who were so brave in the face of other foes, never dared fight these terrible cave-dwellers. They continued to devastate the village, until babies were at a premium, and few to be had at any price; and the only way the people dared to try to circumvent them was by strategy. In time it came about that every house where there were children, or a reasonable hope of them, had secret cubby-holes back of the thick adobe walls; with little doors which shut flush with the wall and were also plastered with adobe, so that when they were shut a stranger—even if he were a sharp-eyed Indian—would never dream of their existence.

19

And whenever arose the dreaded cry, " Here come
the *T'ai-kár-nin!*" the children were hustled
shivering and noiseless, into the secret recesses
and the doors were shut.   Then Mr. Ogre could
come in and peer and sniff about as he liked, bu
no chance to fill his market-basket could he find
And when parents were forced to go away and
leave the babies behind, the poor young ones were
inclosed in their safe but gloomy prisons, and there
in darkness and silence had to await the parenta
home-coming.   These inconveniences were gladly
borne, however, since they preserved the childrer
— and we all know that preserved baby is bette:
than baby-stew.   It was, of course, rather rough
on the Ogres, who began to find all their belts
most distressfully loose; but no one seemed to
consider their feelings.   They were pretty wel
starved when the Spaniards came and delivered
the suffering Isleteños by driving off these savage
neighbors.   This looks suspiciously as if the whole
myth of the Ogres had sprung from the attacks of
the cruel Apaches and Navajos in the old days.

There was one queer thing about these Ogre:
— on their forages they always wore buckskir
masks, just like those of the *Abuelos* of the sacred
dance.   Their bare faces were seen sometimes by
hunters who encountered them on the *llano*, bu
never here in town.   It was in connection with
these masks that Isleta had a great sensation re
cently.   The Hungry Grandfathers had been al
most forgotten, except as a word to change the
minds of children who had about quarter of a mind
to be naughty; but interest was revived by a dis

covery of which my venerable friend Desiderio
Peralta was the hero.

This dear old man — news of his death has come
to me as I write this very chapter — was a remarkable character. He was one of "the oldest inhabitants" of New Mexico — older than any other
Indian among the twelve hundred of Isleta, except
tottering Diego; and that is saying a great deal.
His hair was very gray, and his kindly old face
such an incredible mass of wrinkles that I used to
fancy Father Time himself must have said: "No,
no! You apprentices never do a thing right!
Here, *this* is the way to put on wrinkles!" and that
he then and there took old Desiderio for a model,
and showed the journeymen wrinkle-makers a trick
they never dreamed of. Certainly the job was never
so well done before. From chin to hair-roots,
from ear to ear, was such a crowded, tangled, in-
extricable maze of furrows and cross-harrow lines as
I firmly believe never dwelt together on any other
one human face. Why, Desiderio could have fur-
nished an army of old men with wrinkles! I never
saw him smile without fearing that some of those
wrinkles were going to fall off the edge, so crowded were they at best!

But if his face was *arrugada*, his brain was not.
He was bright and chipper as a young blackbird,
and it was only of late that a touch of rheumatism
took the youth out of his legs. Until recently he
held the important position of Captain of War
for the pueblo; and only two years ago I had the
pleasure of going with two hundred *other* Indians
on a huge rabbit-hunt which was under his per-

sonal supervision, and in which he was as active as any one, both on his feet and with the unerring boomerang. His eyes were good to find about as much through the sights of a rifle as anybody's; and on the whole he was worth a good deal more than I expect to be some seventy years from now. He was a good neighbor, too; and I had few pleasanter hours than those spent in talking with this genial old shrivel, who was *muy sabio* in all the folk-lore and wisdom of his unfathomable race; and very close-mouthed about it, too—as they all are. Still, there were some things which he seemed willing to confide to me; and he always had an attentive listener.

Desiderio was not yet too old to herd his own cattle during the season when they roam abroad; and, while thus engaged, he made a discovery which set the whole quiet village agog, though no other outsider ever heard of it.

One day in 1889 Desiderio started out from the village, driving his cattle. Having steered them across the *acequia* and up the sand-hills to the beginning of the plain, he climbed to the top of the *Kŭ-mai* to watch them through the day—as has been the custom of Isleta herders from time immemorial. In wandering over the rocky top of the peak, he came to a ledge of rocks on the southeast spur of the hill; and there found a fissure, at one end of which was a hole as large as a man's head. Desiderio put his face and his wrinkles down to the hole to see what he could see; and all was dark inside. But if his eyes strained in vain, his ears did not. From far down in the bowels of the mountain came a strange roaring, as of a heavy wind. Desiderio was somewhat dismayed at this; for he knew at once that he had found one of the chimneys of the Ogres; but he did not run away. Hunting around awhile, he found in the fissures of the rocks some ancient buckskin masks—the very ones worn by the Ogres, of course. He put them back, and coming to town straightway told the medicine-men of the Black Eyes—one of the two parties here. They held a *junta;* and after mature deliberation decided to go and get the masks. This was done, and the masks are now treasured in the Black Eye medicine-house.

I have several times carefully explored the *Kú-mai*—a difficult and tiresome task, thanks to the knife-like lava fragments which cover it everywhere, and which will cut a pair of new strong shoes to pieces in an afternoon. It is true that in this hill of bad repute there are several lava-caves, with floors of white sand blown in from the *llano;* and that in these caves there are a few human bones. No doubt some of the savage nomads camped or lived there. None of those famous *ollas* are visible; nor have I ever been able to find any other relics of the Hungry Grandfathers.

XXXI

ALL the animals with which the Tée-wahn are familiar—the buffalo (which they used to hunt on the vast plains to the eastward), the bear, deer, antelope, mountain lion, badger, wild turkey, fox, eagle, crow, buzzard, rabbit, and so on—appear in their legends and fairy tales, as well as in their religious ceremonials and beliefs. Too-whây-deh, the Coyote,[1] or little prairie wolf, figures in countless stories, and always to his own disadvantage. Smart as he is in some things, he believes whatever is told him; and by his credulity becomes the butt of all the other animals, who never tire of "April-fooling" him. He is also a great coward. To call an Indian here "*Too-whây-deh*" is one of the bitterest insults that can be offered him.

[1] Pronounced Coy-óh-ty.

You have already heard how the Coyote fared· at the hands of the fun-loving Bear, and of the Crows and the Blackbirds. A very popular tale is that of his adventure with a bright cousin of his.

Once upon a time Too-wháy-shur-wée-deh, the Little-Blue-Fox,[1] was wandering near a pueblo, and chanced to come to the threshing-floors, where a great many crows were hopping. Just then the Coyote passed, very hungry; and while yet far off, said: "Ai! how the stomach cries! I will just eat Little-Blue-Fox." And coming, he said:

"Now, Little-Blue-Fox, you have troubled me enough! You are the cause of my being chased by the dogs and people, and now I will pay you. I am going to eat you up this very now!"

"No, Coyote-friend," answered the Little-Blue-Fox, "*don't* eat me up! I am here guarding these chickens, for there is a wedding in yonder house, which is my master's, and these chickens are for the wedding-dinner. Soon they will come for the chickens; and will invite me to the dinner—and you can come also."

"Well," said the Coyote, "if *that* is so, I will not eat you, but will help you watch the chickens." So he lay down beside him.

At this, Little-Blue-Fox was troubled, thinking how to get away; and at last he said:

"Friend Too-wháy-deh, I make strange that they have not before now come for the chickens. Perhaps they have forgotten. The best way is for

---

1 He is always a hero, and as smart as the Coyote is stupid. His beautiful pelt is an important part of the costume worn in many of the sacred dances of the Tée-wahn.

me to go to the house and see what the servants are doing."

"It is well," said the Coyote. "Go, then, and I will guard the chickens for you."

So the Little-Blue-Fox started toward the house; but getting behind a small hill, he ran away with fast feet. When it was a good while, and he did not come back, the Coyote thought: "While he is gone, I will give myself some of the chickens." Crawling up on his belly to the threshing-floor, he gave a great leap. But the chickens were only crows, and they flew away. Then he began to say evil of the Little-Blue-Fox for giving him a trick, and started on the trail, vowing: "I will eat him up wherever I catch him."

After many miles he overtook the Little-Blue-Fox, and with a bad face said: "Here! Now I am going to eat you up!"

The other made as if greatly excited, and answered: "No, friend Coyote! Do you not hear that *tombé*[1]?"

The Coyote listened, and heard a drum in the pueblo.

"Well," said the Little-Blue-Fox, "I am called for that dance,[2] and very soon they will come for me. Won't you go too?"

"If that is so, I will not eat you, but we will go to the dance." And the Coyote sat down and began to comb his hair and to make himself pretty with face-paint. When no one came, the Little-Blue-Fox said:

1 Pronounced tom-báy. The sacred drum used in Pueblo dances.
2 In all such Indian dances the participants are named by the officials.

"THERE THEY STOOD SIDE BY SIDE."

"Friend Coyote, I make strange that the *al-guazil* does not come. It is best for me to go up on this hill, whence I can see into the village. You wait here."

"He will not dare to give me another trick," thought the Coyote. So he replied: "It is well. But do not forget to call me."

So the Little-Blue-Fox went up the hill; and as soon as he was out of sight, he began to run for his life.

Very long the Coyote waited; and at last, being tired, went up on the hill — but there was no one there. Then he was very angry, and said: "I will follow him, and eat him surely! *Nothing* shall save him!" And finding the trail, he began to follow as fast as a bird.

Just as the Little-Blue-Fox came to some high cliffs, he looked back and saw the Coyote coming over a hill. So he stood up on his hind feet and put his fore paws up against the cliff, and made many groans, and was as if much excited. In a moment came the Coyote, very angry, crying: "Now you shall not escape me! I am going to eat you up now — now!"

"Oh, no, friend Too-wháy-deh!" said the other; "for I saw this cliff falling down, and ran to hold it up. If I let go, it will fall and kill us both. But come, help me to hold it."

Then the Coyote stood up and pushed against the cliff with his fore paws, very hard; and there they stood side by side. .

Time passing so, the Little-Blue-Fox said:

"Friend Too-wháy-deh, it is long that I am

holding up the cliff, and I am very tired and thirsty. You are fresher. So you hold up the cliff while I go and hunt water for us both; for soon you too will be thirsty. There is a lake somewhere on the other side of this mountain; I will find it and get a drink, and then come back and hold up the cliff while you go."

The Coyote agreed, and the Little-Blue-Fox ran away over the mountain till he came to the lake, just as the moon was rising.

But soon the Coyote was very tired and thirsty, for he held up the cliff with all his might. At last he said: "Ai! how hard it is! I am so thirsty that I will go to the lake, even if I die!"

So he began to let go of the cliff, slowly, slowly — until he held it only with his finger-nails; and then he made a great jump away backward, and ran as hard as he could to a hill. But when he looked around and saw that the cliff did not fall, he was very angry, and swore to eat Too-wháy-shur-wée-deh the very minute he should catch him.

Running on the trail, he came to the lake; and there the Little-Blue-Fox was lying on the bank, whining as if greatly excited. "Now I *will* eat you up, this minute!" cried the Coyote. But the other said: "No, Friend Too-wháy-deh! Don't eat *me* up! I am waiting for some one who can swim as well as you can. I just bought a big cheese[1] from a shepherd to share with you; but when I went to drink, it slipped out of my hands into the water.

---

[1] Of course chickens and cheeses were not known to the Pueblos before the Spanish conquest; and the cheese is so vital a part of the story that I hardly think it can be an interpolation. So this tale, though very old, is probably not ancient—that is, it has been invented since 1600.

"'HOW SHALL I GET IT?' SAID THE COYOTE."

Come here, and I will show you." He took the Coyote to the edge of the high bank, and pointed to the moon in the water.

"M — m!" said the Coyote, who was fainting with hunger. "But how shall I get it? It is very deep in the water, and I shall float up before I can dive to it."

"That is true, friend," said the other. "There is but one way. We must tie some stones to your neck, to make you heavy so you can go down to it."

So they hunted about until they found a buck-skin thong and some large stones; and the Little-Blue-Fox tied the stones to the Coyote's neck, the Coyote holding his chin up, to help.

"Now, friend Too-wháy-deh, come here to the edge of the bank and stand ready. I will take you by the back and count *weem, wée-si, p'áh-chu!* And when I say *three,* you must jump and I will push — for now you are very heavy."

So he took the Coyote by the back of the neck, swaying him back and forth as he counted. And at *"p'áh-chu!"* he pushed hard, and the Coyote jumped, and went into the deep water, and — never came out again!

XXXII

DOCTOR FIELD-MOUSE

IT was the evening of the 14th of March. In the valley of the Rio Grande, that stands at the end of the winter. Now it is to open the big mother-canal that comes from the river to all the fields, giving them to drink after their long thirst; and now to plow the *milpas*, and to uncover the buried grape-vines, and make ready for the farmer's work.

As the door opened to admit stalwart Francisco to the big flickering room where we were all sitting in silence, the long, shrill wail of a Coyote, away up on the Accursed Hill, blew in after him on the boisterous March wind. The boys pricked up their ears; and bright-faced Manuelito[1] turned to his white-headed grandfather, and said:

" *Tata*, why is it that Too-wháy-deh always howls so? Perhaps he has a pain; for he has been crying ever since the beginning of the world —as they told us in the story of the Fawns and the She-Wolf."

"What, Unknowing!" answered the old man, kindly. "Hast thou never heard of the Coyote's

1 Pronounced Mahn-way-lée-to.

toothache, and who was the first medicine-man in all the world? It is not well not to know that; for from that comes all that we know to cure the sick. And for that, I will tell—but it is the last story of the year. For to-morrow is *Tu-shée-wim*, the Spring Medicine-Dance; and the snakes are coming out from their winter houses. After that, we must not tell of the Things of Old. For it is very long ago; and if one made a mistake in telling, and said that which was not all true, *Ch'áh-rah-ráh-deh* would bite him, and he would die.[1] But this one I will tell thee."

In the First Days, when the people had broken through the crust of the earth, and had come up out of their dark prison, underground, and crossed Shee-p'ah-póon, the great Black Lake of Tears, they came to the shore on this side. Then it came that all the animals were made; and very soon the Coyote was sent by the Trues to carry a buckskin bag far south, and not to open it until he should come to the Peak of the White Clouds. For many days he ran south, with the bag on his back. But there was nothing to eat, and he grew very hungry. At last he thought: "Perhaps in this bag there is to eat." So he took it from his back, and untied the thongs, and looked in. But there was nothing in it except the stars; and as soon as the bag was opened they all flew up into the sky, where they are to this day.

[1] A fixed belief among the Pueblos, who will tell none of their myths between the Spring Medicine-Making, in March, and the Fall Medicine-Making, in October, lest the rattlesnake punish them for some slip from the truth.

When the Trues saw that Too-whảy-deh had disobeyed, they were angry, and made it that his punishment should be to wander up and down forever, howling with the toothache and finding no rest.

So Too-whảy-deh went out with his toothache, running all over the world groaning and crying; and when the other four-feet slept he could only sit and howl. Because he came to talk with the other animals, if they could not cure him, they caught the toothache too; and that is the reason why they sometimes cry. But none have it like the Coyote, who can find no rest.

In those times there were no medicine-men in the world,— not even of the people,— and the animals found no cure.

Time passing so, it came one day that T'hoo-chée-deh, the smallest of Mice, who lives in the little mounds around the chapparo-bush, was making his road underground, when he came to a kind of root with a sweet smell. T'hoo-chée-deh was very wise; and he took the root, and put it with others in a buckskin pouch he carried under his left arm.

In a few days Kee-oo-ée-deh, the Prairie-Dog, came with his head all fat with toothache, and said:

"Friend Field-Mouse, can you not cure me of this pain? For all say you are very wise with herbs."

"I do not know," answered T'hoo-chée-deh. "But we will try. For I have found a new root, and perhaps it is good."

So he mixed it with other roots, all pounded, and put it on the cheek of Kee-oo-ée-deh; and in a little, the toothache was gone.

In that time it was that there was so much

toothache among the animals that the Mountain Lion, Commander of Beasts, called a council to see what should be done.   When every kind that walks on the ground had met, he asked each of them if they had found no cure; but none of them knew any.   The Coyote was there, howling with pain; but all the other sick were at home.

At last it was to the Field-Mouse, who is the smallest of all animals, and who did not wish to seem wise until all the greater ones had spoken. When the Mountain Lion said, "And thou, T'hoo-chée-deh—hast thou a cure?" he rose in his place and came forward modestly, saying: " If the others will allow me, and with the help of the Trues, I will try what I found last."

Then he drew from his left-hand bag the roots one by one; and last of all, the root of the *chee-ma-hár*, explaining what it had done for Kee-oo-ée-deh.   He pounded it to powder with a stone, and mixed it with fat; and spreading it on flat leaves, put it to the Coyote's jaw.   And in a little the pain was gone.[1]

At that the Mountain Lion, the Bear, the Buffalo, and all the other Captains of Four-feet, declared T'hoo-chée-deh the Father-of-All-Medicine. They made a strong law that from that time the body of the Field-Mouse should be held sacred, so that no animal dares to kill him or even to touch him dead.   And so it remains to this day.   But only the

[1] This cure is still practised among the Tée-wahn. The sovereign remedy for toothache, however, is to go to the *estufa* after dark, carrying food in the left hand, march round inside the big circular room three times, leave the food under the secret recess in the wall where the scalps taken in old wars are kept, and then come out. The toothache is always left behind!

birds and the snakes, who were not at the Council of
the Four feet, they do not respect T'hoo-chée-deh.

So the Field-Mouse was the first medicine-man.
He chose one of each kind of four-feet to be his
assistants, and taught them the use of all herbs,
and how to cure pain, so that each might practise
among his own people—a Bear-doctor for the
Bears, and a Wolf-doctor for the Wolves, and so to
all the tribes of the animals.

Of those he taught, there was one who was not
a True Believer—the Badger. But he listened
also, and made as if he believed all. With time,
the teaching was done; and T'hoo-chée-deh sent
all his assistant doctors home to their own peoples
to heal. But whenever one of them was asked
with the sacred corn-meal[1] to come and cure a sick
one, he always came first to get the Father, the
Field-Mouse, to accompany and help him.

But all this time Kahr-naí-deh, the Badger, was
not believing; and at last he said to his wife:

" Now I will *see* if Old T'hoo-chée-deh is really a
medicine-man. If he finds me, I will believe him."

So from that day for four days the Badger
touched no food, until he was almost dead. And
on the fifth day he said:

"*Tn-hlee-oo wáy-ee*, wife of me, go now and call
T'hoo-chée-deh, to see if he will cure me."

So the Badger-wife went with meal to the house
of the Field-Mouse, making to be very sad; and
brought him back with her. When they came, the
Badger was as if very sick and in great pain.

---

[1] The necessary accompaniment, among the Pueblos, of a call for the
doctor. In some cases, the sacred smoking-herb was used. Either article
was wrapped in corn-husk. See, also, "Some Strange Corners of Our
Country," chapters xviii and xx.

T'hoo-chée-deh asked nothing; but took off the little pouch of roots and laid it beside him. And then rubbing a little wood-ashes on his hands, he put them on the stomach and breast of the Badger, rubbing and feeling. When he had felt the Badger's stomach, he began to sing:

Káhr-nah-hlóo-hlee wee-end-t'hú
Beh-hú hoo-báhn,
Ah-náh káh-chah-him-aí
T'hóo-chee-hlóo-hlee t'oh-ah-yin-áhb
Wee-end-t'hú beh-hú hoo-báhn.

(Badger-Old-Man four days
Has the hunger-killing,
To know, to know surely
If Field-Mouse-Old-Man
Has the Medicine Power.
Four days, four days,
He has the hunger-killing.)

When he had finished rubbing and singing, he said to the Badger:

"There is no need of a remedy. In my teaching I found you attentive—now be true. You have wasted, in trying my power. Now get up and eat, to make up for the lost. And do not think that way again."

With that, he took his pouch of roots and went home. As soon as he was out of the house, the Badger said to his wife:

"My wife, now I believe that Mouse-Old-Man *has* the Power; and never again will I think *that* way."

Then the Badger-wife brought food, and he ate—for he was dying of hunger. When he had eaten, the animals came in to see him, for they had heard that he was very sick. He told them all

that had been, and how T'hoo-chée-deh had known
his trick.   At that, all the animals were afraid of
the Field-Mouse, and respected him more than ever
— for it was plain that he indeed had the Power.

Time passing so, it came that one day the Men
of the Old made *nah-kú-ah-shu*, the great round-
hunt.   When they had made a great circle on the
llano, and killed many rabbits, some of them found
T'hoo-chée-deh, and made him prisoner.   They
brought him before the *principales*, who questioned
him, saying:

"How do you gain your life?"

"I gain it," he answered, "by going about
among the animals who are sick, and curing
them."

Then the elders said: "If that is so, teach us
your Power, and we will set you free; but if not,
you shall die."

T'hoo-chée-deh agreed, and they brought him
to town with honor.   For twelve days and twelve
nights he and the men stayed shut up in the *estufa;*
for two days fasting, and one day making the medicine-dance, and then fasting and then dancing
again, as our medicine-men do to this day.

On the last night, when he had taught the men
all the herbs and how to use them, and they had
become wise with practice, they sent T'hoo-chée-
deh out with a strong guard, that nothing should
harm him.   They set him down at the door of his
own house under the chapparo.   A law was made,
giving him full liberty of all that is grown in the
fields.   To this day, all True Believers honor him,
so that he is not called small any more.   When
they sing of him in the sacred places, they make

his house great, calling it *koor-óo-hlee naht-hóo*, the Mountain of the Chapparo. And him they call not T'hoo-chée-deh, the Field-Mouse, but *Pee-íd-deh p'ah-hláh-queer*, the Deer-by-the-River, that he may not seem of little honor.[1] For he was the Father of Medicine, and taught us how to cure the sick.

"*Tahb-kóon-ahm?*" cried the boys. "Is *that* why the Coyote always cries? And is that why we must never hurt the Field-Mouse, but show him respect, as to elders?"

"That is the very why," said Manuelito's grandfather, gravely; and all the old men nodded.

"And why—" began 'Tonio. But his father shook his head.

"*Tah!* It is enough. *Tóo-kwai!*"

So we stepped out into the night to our homes. And from the *Kú-mai*, black against the starry sky, the howl of Too-wháy-deh, wandering with his toothache, swelled across the sleeping village of the Tée-wahn.

[1] This is not an exception. Nearly all the animals known to the Tée-wahn have not only their common name, but a ceremonial and sacred one, which is used exclusively in the songs and rites.